Curvy Fake Wife for the Player

A Single Dad & the Nanny Fake Marriage Romance

Piper Sullivan

Copyright © 2024 by Piper Sullivan

All rights reserved.

No part of this book may be reproduced in any form or by any electronic or mechanical means, including information storage and retrieval systems, without written permission from the author, except for the use of brief quotations in a book review.

Enjoy Spicy Romances?

Download Safeguarded for FREE Now!

Chapter 1

Alex

"I'm serious, Alex, you need to stay out of trouble. Just, I don't know, stay inside and have a beer, maybe watch a movie where a lot of shit gets blown up."

I could hear the frustration and the seriousness in my agent, Jack's voice. It was serious, I knew that, but I was Alex Witter, top winger for the Houston Highlanders, I didn't take anything too seriously except my career.

"I don't get into trouble, Jack. It just seems to find me." That was truer than I wanted it to be. "I just got back from visiting Dante, so you shouldn't hear anything about me other than I wore a feather boa while I had a tea party with a little girl."

The trip to visit Dante had actually been fun and relaxing. The best part? Other than adoring fans, no one bothered me while I was there.

"'That's good. Very good."

"Worried?" Jack had been my agent for nearly a decade, I kept him on because he made me a very rich man with incredible endorsement deals and he always gave it to me straight, even the bad news. Maybe especially the bad news.

"Hell yeah, I'm worried. Top scorer in the League or not, another fuck up could cost you twenty million worth of endorsement deals. We have three contracts that renew this year, Alex."

Shit. "This is bullshit, Jack. I didn't force Tatiana to talk to the tabloids about our sex life." My ex, one of many, had hoped that her little stunt would get me to call her or rekindle our brief fling, or some such nonsense. She was dead wrong.

"Maybe so, but your name was connected to some acts most wouldn't consider family friendly."

"Yeah well I'm not a family man, am I?"

"No," Jack sighed. "You know how these morality clauses work, man. Keep your shit under wraps and stop fucking crazy."

I barked out a laugh at his advice. "Hard to do when you're me." It was how I always justified things that happened to me. But I took my job on the ice completely seriously, and the privileged life it gave me. "I won't do anything to screw up my business, but I can't be responsible for what other people do."

"You could stop sticking your dick in crazy, Alex.

Training starts in a few weeks and I want you fresh and not distracted by anything. Feel me?"

I nodded even though he couldn't see me. "I feel ya, and I'll keep that in mind," I promised and ended the call.

I'd come too far in my life, from a dirt poor kid who grew up in a trailer park in Crayfish Hills, Tennessee to the number one high school, and then college prospect, before becoming the top scorer in the National Hockey League. I wouldn't let a spurned woman ruin it all because she wanted more than I ever promised her. Fuck that. I loved my life. Some might consider it empty, the women and the parties, the vacations and the money, but it was exactly the life I wanted. The media called me Hockey's Millionaire Playboy, and to a certain extent, I played up the role for their sake. The fans ate it up, the women loved it too, and as long as I didn't go too far, management was fine with my antics. I made headlines both on and off the ice, and there had never been any problems with that.

Until now. Fucking Tatiana. Jack was right about one thing, I had to stop sticking my dick in crazy before it caught up to me in a really bad way.

"I guess I'm staying inside," I said out loud to myself as I made my way to the kitchen, pulling a beer from the fridge along with a pack of steaks.

My chef had left a few meals, but I was in the mood for something simple, so I seasoned the steaks, grabbed two more beers, and took the elevator to the roof. I lived in a penthouse apartment but the roof made it feel like a house with the grill area in one corner, plants and flowers all along the perimeter, and comfortable seating with a great view of all of Houston. Enjoying the last hour of sunshine of the day while I ate helped me relax. As much as I'd wanted to hunt down Tatiana and tell her off, I was glad my first instinct had been to call Jack. He'd gotten me a new phone number so she couldn't call, and planted stories that she was just jealous that I'd moved on before she did.

The truth was there was nothing to move on from. We met at a charity event and hit it off immediately, and by hit it off, I mean that we were instantly attracted to one another. She was interested and easy, which was exactly how I liked my women. I was interested and horny, and we'd spent a hot and adventurous week in bed together before we came up for air. We had our first date on day nine, and by day eleven I realized my mistake and broke things off with her. That was a year ago, and now that she was aging out of the modeling world, she was using me to stay relevant.

"Stop," I growled to myself as I finished off the steak and the second beer. She wasn't worth thinking about, but I gave in to a few more thoughts as I made my way back down to the apartment and then banished all thoughts of her from my mind completely. I needed to focus on the upcoming season. I needed to be ready, to be sharp. There were always young players looking to steal my spotlight, and the closer I got to thirty, the harder the young bucks pushed. I wasn't ready to give up hockey yet, which meant I needed to focus.

I grabbed another beer from the fridge, because when training started I would only indulge in alcohol on the weekends, and never more than two drinks until the season was over, which wouldn't be for a good long while if we made the playoffs for the sixth season in a row.

* * *

That third beer had knocked me on my ass, or maybe it was the sun and the stress. Whatever the reason was, I woke up to a moonlit sky. I didn't usually sleep in the middle of the day because there was always too much to do, but I'd been laying low since Tatiana's interview had brought the paparazzi vultures to my front door once again.

I rolled off the sofa to go in search of dinner, but a whimpering sound stopped me. I lived in a penthouse apartment so it wasn't as if there was a stray animal inside, but I went to check the roof since critters sometimes found themselves stuck up there. A quick look around revealed nothing, so I shrugged it off and went back downstairs. The whimper came again and once again, I frowned.

"What in the hell is that?"

I had no idea how a stray animal could have made it all the way up to my floor without being noticed, but the sound wouldn't quit, so I opened the front door and froze.

A baby sat in a hot pink carrier on my doorstep. I looked up and down the hall, waiting for one of my players to jump out and take credit for this obvious prank, but there was no one there. No one but the whimpering baby kicking her chubby little legs in the air.

"Where did you come from?" It was a good damn question but since the hall appeared to be empty, I had no choice but to pick up the carrier holding the baby and bring it inside.

I set the carrier on the kitchen counter and stared at the tiny thing with a shock of red hair and big green eyes. How did a baby end up on my doorstep? Mine was the only unit on this floor and it required a special key card to gain penthouse access.

I picked up the phone on the wall that connected me immediately with the doorman. "Barry, has anyone been to my floor today?"

"No, sir. A few photographers tried to gain access but I got rid of 'em. Is there a problem?"

"I'm not sure yet. I'll let you know." I ended the call and turned back to the baby and the small bag hooked onto her carrier. There had to be some information on this baby somewhere. Right? Inside, there were a few diapers, baby bottles, and the smallest clothes I'd ever seen. Past the baby wipes and a tube of ointment was nothing except the bottom of the bag.

"Dammit."

"Ba-ba-ba-ba." The baby babbled with a watery smile as she kicked her legs like she was trying to tell me something. She kicked again and that's when I heard it, the crinkle of paper. Behind her kicking legs, I found a note.

Alex,

I'd like you to meet your daughter. She has your eyes, don't you think?

Before you curse me to hell and back, read this letter all the way through. She's yours and I have no doubts about that, but if you do, have a DNA test if you don't believe me.

Don't bother trying to track me down because I'll be dead by the time you find me, that's why I'm leaving her with you.

Please, take care of our little girl, give her a good life and make sure she knows I loved her more than anything.

I know you don't think you have it in you to be a father, to be responsible for someone so tiny, but I know that you do. Take care of her, and yourself.

That was all the note said, she hadn't signed it or anything. A ball of acid formed in the pit of my stomach as the situation started to sink in.

A baby.

Someone had left a baby on my doorstep and said she was mine. It couldn't be true. It had to be a play for cash. It was the only thing that made sense.

A loud cry tore from her little body and in a panic, I unfastened the harness around her and pulled her into my arms.

"It's all right, little girl. I'll figure this out." I had no choice. This was exactly the kind of fuck up Jack had warned me about.

It took a few minutes to settle her down but when she

stopped crying, I put her back in the carrier. She started crying again right away.

    We played this game for an hour before it became clear that she wouldn't go back to the carrier. She was tiny and soft and smelled so sweet, which was probably how she got me to hold her all night.

Chapter 2

Sasha

Serenity stood with a smile when I entered her lavish office at Elite Nanny Service.

"Sasha, I'm so glad you could make it in today. Have a seat and tell me, how are you doing?"

I couldn't help but smile at Serenity Majors. She was a beautiful woman with insane curves and an impeccable fashion sense. She looked like she belonged on the streets of New York City, not running a nanny agency in Houston. She was kind and nurturing, treating all of us as if we were members of her family.

"Hey, Serenity, you look fabulous as always."

"This old thing?" She laughed and brushed off my words with a smile and a blush. "So?"

"I'm good," I answered as I took the plush white chair in front of her desk. "I'm going to miss Jenna and James, but I'm so proud of them and happy for them." The twins

I'd been working with since they were one had officially started first grade and I was no longer needed. It was part of the job but that didn't make it hurt any less to say goodbye. "How are you?"

"Oh, you know. Busy as always but I love it." She flashed a beaming smile and laid her hand over a stack of files. "I have a few new families that might be a good fit for you. Interested or do you need a break?"

I took a moment to think about my answer. The truth was I hadn't been back to Connecticut to visit my family in more than a year, but that wasn't because I didn't have the time or the funds. It was because I didn't want to, not really. My family was complicated and that was putting it mildly so staying away was best for everyone, but most especially my mental health.

"That depends on what you have for me," I answered.

Whatever Serenity was about to say was paused when the door behind me slammed open. I was on my feet in an instant, practically jumping over the glass desk to get behind my boss. My heart raced as I took in the giant blond man with broad shoulders and let out a shriek that brought all the attention to me.

"Who are you? What the hell are you doing, bursting in here like that?" My voice sounded shrill and anxious, but that's exactly what I felt. The large man had crazed green eyes, and if not for the baby strapped to his body, he would've looked more terrifying simply due to his size.

He was at least six feet, possibly six and a half feet, with broad shoulders, long, strong legs, and a power that emanated from him. That power was intimidating but it was also awesome. His gaze landed on Serenity.

"You have to help me." My heart still raced as Serenity stood and smoothed her hands over her red dress.

"Have a seat, sir. I'm guessing you're new to parenthood?"

He nodded as his wild eyes darted around the room, the baby smiling and babbling against his chest. Finally, the big man sat and let out a long, expansive breath.

"Less than twenty-four hours, in fact. The baby is good, perfect as long as I keep her in my arms, but the minute I put her down? She howls like a banshee."

Serenity laughed and put a hand to her chest as she settled a sweet gaze on the man and the little baby with a fiery crown of hair. His blond brows dipped into a dark scowl.

"It's no laughing matter. I need help, and my friend says you are the best."

"I love to hear that. Who is your friend?"

"Dante Rush. You found him a nanny recently."

She nodded and walked around the desk, sitting on the edge with a grin. "If you know Dante then you know how I do things."

The man wasn't interested in the details, that was obvious by the set of his shoulders and the look of determination in green eyes that were exactly the same as the adorable baby girl fixed against his chest.

"I didn't get the details from him, but I can afford your fees and I'll pay it without negotiating. Please." Unlike so many of the entitled parents I've met and worked with over the years, this man had more of an air of desperation than entitlement. The baby started to cry in his arms, but as she started fussing, he pulled her closer, jostling her gently. "Please."

Serenity reached out and let one finger graze the soft tuft of red hair on the baby's head. "Sasha, you think you can take this sweetheart while I have a talk with Mr.?"

"Witter," he answered nervously, eyes darting back and forth. "Alex Witter." I noticed that Serenity's gaze flashed at the name as if it was familiar to her, but to me, he was just another handsome Texan, and my focus was on the baby girl in his arms. I stared at the man a beat too long before her words registered.

"Oh, sure." It was clear the man wasn't an actual threat, so I relaxed and slowly made my way towards the blond giant, still wary but willing to help out. "Hey, sweet girl. I'm Sasha." I talked gently to the baby who turned her big green eyes to me, curious at first, and then smiling excitedly. "That's right. I'm Sasha and we're going to hang out for a bit." I smiled at her and her smile grew as baby babble spilled from her rosebud lips.

When I reached for her, the man, Alex Witter, gripped her tight as if he was reluctant to let her go. "Careful. She tends to get a little fussy," he began when I scooped her from his arms and nestled her close.

"I'll be damned. How did you do that?" His deep voice with a hint of a southern accent that was miles away from Texas was filled with awe. I smiled at the man and really wished I hadn't, because this close, he wasn't just handsome. He was breathtaking with green eyes, dotted with gold and dark gold specks. His skin held a hint of a tan like he spent a lot of time outdoors, his pink lips were full and his mouth, wide and kissable. Wait, what? No, not kissable. Just noticeably plump.

"This is what I do, Mr. Witter." I glanced around in search of a diaper bag, but when I found none, I held the baby closer and rushed from the office. Curiosity burned in my gut at the situation that brought the blond Viking to Elite Nanny Service.

He was clearly out of place, not to mention out of his depths as a father, but why? Why was he so out of sorts? Was this the first time he'd been left alone with the child? I took the baby to one of the meeting rooms stocked with everything a kid from aged one month to five years might need and changed her diaper.

"You're a good little girl," I cooed while she kept up a steady stream of baby babble as I changed her, punching those chubby little legs as if she was going somewhere.

The big guy was a little on the gruff side, but it was clear that whatever landed this little girl on his doorstep, he cared about her. It made me think of my own father, rich and short-tempered. He would have taken to raging at this little girl to get her to settle down. The idea of reaching out for professional help never would have occurred to him.

"I guess in that way, you're lucky." She laughed and

continued kicking wildly. "I hope you have a really great life, sweet girl. I really do."

If her father was here, it meant he could afford to give her the best life had to offer, which made me smile. With the right start in life, a child could go far, and though I barely knew her, that's what I hoped for this little girl.

Chapter 3

Alex

I stared across the desk at the well-dressed woman with a kind smile and thick sable hair, deciding whether or not to reveal all of my secrets to her. It was hard *not* to trust her when she looked at me as if she somehow understood everything I was going through. "Okay," I sighed and shook my head. "Someone dropped her on my doorstep last night with a note that said she was mine."

"Do you know who the mother is?" She asked without judgment, which was what I really needed.

"No," I sighed and scrubbed a hand over my face. "She said she was dying and that she would be gone by the time I tracked her down, which takes a money grab off the table. *If* all of that is true, anyway." It was naïve, no, it was silly of me to reveal all of my secrets to a virtual stranger without asking her to sign a non-disclosure agreement. Jack was going to have my ass when he found out, and then he'd chew it up and spit it out when he heard everything.

Serenity sat back in her white leather seat and grinned. "I'm well aware of who you are, Mr. Witter and I can assure you that I have a reputation for being discreet."

My shoulders relaxed at her words. "That's good. But I have to warn you that my agent will probably come around in a few days with NDAs for you and the woman to sign."

She waved off my words with a laugh. "I can handle him, I assure you."

That was good because she would have to. "But, can you help me with my current predicament?" I looked over my shoulder at the door where the curvy raven-haired woman had exited from with my daughter. *Maybe* daughter my conscience corrected automatically. The DNA test was next on my list, just as soon as I could find some good help.

"I can."

"Good." I nodded and sat up a little taller, feeling more self-assured than I had since the little bundle of baby arrived on my doorstep. "I want her, the woman who has my daughter right now. She got her to stop crying."

She laughed. At me. No one ever laughed at Alex Witter. At least, not anymore. "You are lucky because Sasha has recently become available, but I'll have to check with her to see if she's willing to take on a job like this."

I frowned. "What does that mean? She's good with the

baby and she doesn't know who I am. I want her. It has to be her."

Serenity nodded. "Okay, assuming Sasha is available, what exactly are your needs?"

"I have no idea. I start training soon and I need someone who can be with her during the day while I'm training and to help me at night, at least until I get used to the responsibilities of fatherhood." A dark scowl crossed my face. "I sound like an asshole, right? If she's with the girl day and night, when will she sleep?"

She stood and placed a hand on my shoulder. It wasn't a come on or anything tawdry, it was just affectionate, possibly with a hint of pity. "There are live-in nannies, Mr. Witter."

"Alex. Call me Alex."

She nodded and took the chair right beside me. "A live-in nanny sounds like what you need, but I'll still need you to outline your needs so that Sasha can make an informed decision."

"Yeah, okay. This is all new to me. I don't know any babies, except my goddaughter and I'm more of an uncle. Not a father. I need help learning how to be a father as well as someone to take care of her while I'm away." At least until paternity was confirmed. After that? Hell, I had no idea.

"Sasha is one of my best, so if she decides to take this assignment she will be a valuable guide through parenthood for you."

I nodded because that was exactly what I needed. A guide. A daddy coach. "Perfect. I need her. Now."

"You're used to getting everything you want right when you want it, Mr. Witter."

"Yes." There was no point pretending otherwise.

"I understand but Sasha has a say in this as well."

Of course she did. "I'll double the pay."

Serenity's eyes widened in shock. "That may not be necessary. My nannies are paid very well."

"It is necessary," I insisted, feeling more confident as the words tumbled out of my mouth. "She doesn't know who I am yet, but you do. You know that in addition to the child, she will have to deal with tabloid journalists, paparazzi and wannabe groupies. She is definitely going to earn her salary, I promise that. Double the pay up front and if she wants or needs something else to do this, please tell me." I sounded like a desperate ass which was never a good negotiating position but I was desperate. I'd hardly gotten any sleep last night because I couldn't put the baby down without her bursting into tears. Sure, I dozed a few times in the recliner but anxiety made it difficult to get a good rest. I was desperate and willing to pay anything, hell to do just about anything to get that woman to be my nanny.

"So you're accepting paternity of the child?"

"For now, I am. I will have a rush done on paternity to make certain that she's mine but right now she needs to be cared for, so as right now, she's mine."

That seemed to please the woman because she

unleashed a smile that was full of pride and satisfaction. "I'll talk to Sasha and have an answer for you before the end of business today."

I wanted to tell her that wasn't good enough, that I didn't just need an answer *now,* but that I needed to take that woman, Sasha, home with me immediately. But there was a steely core to Serenity that was easy to see. She looked soft and feminine but she was no pushover, and I'd end up worse than I was now if I pissed her off.

"Okay, yeah. Thank you, Serenity."

"Don't worry, Alex. I will find you the perfect nanny. I promise."

I didn't have a lot of trust stored up at the moment, but when Serenity made that promise, I believed her. "Then I hope we'll be doing business together very soon."

She stood and walked with me to another room Sasha was singing to my daughter. My baby stared up at her as if she was the most interesting person she had ever seen.

"Oh Alex, I have no doubt that we will."

Chapter 4

Sasha

I stood on the sidewalk before a tall glass and cement building that stretched into the clouds. It was the absolute height of luxury, I could tell as someone who grew up surrounded by wealth, but even I was intimidated by the ostentatious display. It was a nice change of pace from the large mansions with acres of land that stretched in all directions that had dominated my professional life for the past decade, so I decided to embrace the difference.

It won't be so bad.

It couldn't possibly be all that bad since Mr. Witter was determined to pay me double what I'd made for the past five years. Serenity had assured me that I would earn the pay hike with all the extras that came with working for a man like Mr. Witter, but how could I turn down the opportunity to fatten my future savings? I couldn't. There would come a time when my life would no longer accommodate a live-in nanny position, and I would have my savings to fall back on.

And your trust fund, that annoying bitch that lived in my subconscious reminded me the way she always did.

Yes, I had a trust fund, but in all the years since I left Connecticut, I'd only used it once. I lived on my salary and that was that. The fact that it pissed off my dad only made it feel *that much* better.

The day was sunny and warm, but as I stepped into the black and silver marble lobby of Mr. Witter's building, I was instantly hit with a shot of cold air that sent a shiver down my spine. *It's not an omen,* I told myself and put on my best smile for the uniformed doorman with the salt and pepper hair.

"Hi, Barry. I'm Sasha and I'm here for Mr. Witter."

He looked me up and down with a studious gaze that was almost offensive. "You're here for Mr. Witter?"

"I am." I kept my smile in place because that's how I'd been trained my entire life, but the disdain, or maybe it was disbelief, in his grey-green gaze put me on edge.

"I'm sorry, but I can't let you up." He didn't make a call or look at a list, which meant he was simply rejecting me.

"Mind telling me why?"

"Yes, I do mind, actually."

Oh, he wanted to play it that way? Okay. I was used to people treating me a certain way because I was considered 'the help' or because I was a lot curvier than the average woman even down here in Texas, but that didn't mean I tolerated that nonsense. After all, I was Sasha Turner, daughter of the media mogul Bradley Rutherford Turner. No one treated me like that, not because I was someone important, but because I was someone, period.

"What if I told you that Mr. Witter was expecting me?"

Barry tossed his head back and laughed. "You think you're the first woman to try that line with me, sweetheart? You're not, which means you're not going up."

I frowned at his words. Did women often try to get inside Mr. Witter's apartment? I mean sure he was big and classically handsome with his shaggy blond hair and sparkling green eyes, but lying to get into his apartment was a bit much. Wasn't it?

"You should leave before you embarrass yourself, Miss."

That was it, that look of pity in his eyes pissed me off more than I could possibly explain. I leaned across the tall marble counter that kept him separate from the visitors, narrowed my gaze and lowered my voice.

"Look, Barry, I don't know who you think I am or what you think my motives are, and frankly I don't give a shit. But what I can tell you is that if I leave now, I'm not coming back, and if that happens you will be the one out of a job. So please, for both of our sakes, call Mr. Witter and tell him that Sasha Turner is downstairs and she wishes entry to his apartment."

He sized me up for a long minute before deciding to hedge his bets and save his job, picking up the phone and talking discreetly into the receiver.

"Send her up!" Alex barked loud enough that I heard him.

"Right away, sir." Barry turned to me with an apology in his eyes that I chose to ignore. "You have to understand...," he began but I cut him off.

"I understand you have a job to do, but I don't understand you treating me like less than a person based on your own personal opinion."

Without another word, he escorted me to the elevator, inserted a key, and pressed the large P that would take me to the penthouse. "It opens into the hallway and Mr. Witter's door is at the other end."

"Thank you." Just because he was a presumptuous pompous jerk didn't mean I had to be.

The elevator ride to the top lasted several minutes, at least that's what it felt like, or maybe it was just my nerves at starting a new job. Or, more likely, it was this particular job for the mysterious, handsome man who seemingly had a baby dropped into his lap. I decided on my way here that I wouldn't judge Alex. I didn't know his circumstances, and as far as I could tell, he cared about my new charge. Nothing else was my business.

The doors slid open into a dimly lit hall that was black and silver just like the downstairs lobby. Step by step, I made my way towards the imposing black door, willing my heart to stop beating like this was a cause for worry. This was a job, an assignment like dozens of others I'd had over the years. There was no cause for alarm. Nothing to worry about.

I repeated those words over and over as I rapped on the door in five sharp knocks and waited.

The door flung open immediately and Mr. Witter appeared with wild, frantic eyes as he reached out and grabbed my wrist, yanking me inside.

"Thank god you're here," he growled and then dropped my arm as if he just now realized his faux pas. "Sorry. But I'm glad you're here."

"It's all right. What's the problem?"

"Which one?" He asked around a snort and scrubbed a hand down his face. It was then I noticed that Mr. Witter didn't have a shirt on. His chest and back were smooth and perfectly bronzed, like a statue. Covered in muscles and ink, he was a sight to behold as I followed him towards the sound of a baby crying. "This is the problem." He stepped aside and motioned towards the overstuffed sofa where the little girl laid on her back, naked with her feet kicking in the air.

I should have bitten back the laughter, but it fell free before I could compose myself. Three discarded diapers dotted the sofa, each one more mangled than the previous.

"You've never changed a diaper."

"No." His answer was simple and plain, no excuses. I appreciated that.

"First, your sofa is far too nice to double as a changing table." But since it seemed that fatherhood was thrust upon him, I decided to cut him a break. "Do you have more diapers?"

"A few," he grumbled and handed me one. "They're tricky. Good luck."

I smiled at him and then down at the little girl who wore a sweet smile. "Okay, Mr. Witter, at first this seems impossible, but after two or three diaper changes, you'll see it's nothing." To prove my point, I grabbed the baby at her ankles and slid the diaper underneath her, making use of the diaper ointment and baby powder on the coffee table beside me. "Front flap up, left sticker and then right sticker, and there you go!" I lifted the baby in the air, her legs and arms kicking as she cooed sweetly. "Fresh as a daisy."

"How did you do that?" His green eyes were wide with shock, a look of awe on his face.

"Like I said, it's easy once you know what you're doing. You'll catch on," I assured him as my gaze raked over his naked torso.

He seemed to realize just now that he was half naked. "She squirmed and nearly rolled off the sofa when I removed the dirty diaper and I didn't want her to fall."

I chuckled at his dismay. "That's why you need a changing table."

"I don't know what that is," he admitted easily, something I noticed that rich and powerful men had a hard time doing. "Make a list of what she needs. Please," he added belatedly.

I wanted to ask—badly—what in the hell had

happened that led to a clear bachelor taking care of a baby, but again, it wasn't my business. "I'll do that, and maybe you can do something for me?"

He frowned as he raked one hand, and then the other, through his thick blond hair. "What's that?"

"Tell me her name. Babies respond better when they have a familiar word to answer to."

His brows furrowed. "I don't know. When she arrived, she didn't have one." His cheeks turned a bright shade of pink and he shook his head. "It's complicated, but I guess I have to give her a name?"

I didn't want to add to his guilt or whatever else he was feeling, so I only nodded. "What did she come with?" It looked as if I would have to dive right into whatever this messy situation was, and it was lucky for Mr. Witter and his little girl that I handled messy like a pro.

"Just the bag," he said and pointed to a pale blue bag covered in daisies. "It had a few baby items in it, but that was it."

"No note?"

"Attached to the carrier," he said absently.

The more pieces of the puzzle were revealed to me, the greater my sympathy for this situation became. "Do you mind?" I asked and pointed to the bag.

He nodded.

I went through the bag to see if there was anything he'd forgotten, because in my experience even the most detail oriented man tended to miss important things right in front of his face. I took inventory of what was left and it wasn't much, about five diapers, two bottles pre-filled with formula, a fresh pack of baby wipes, and a few onesies.

"Told you there was nothing."

I looked up at him with a smile as the little girl's head fell against my shoulder. "Did you check all the pockets?" I didn't wait for an answer as I dug into the smaller zippered areas and found a pacifier with a plastic sunflower on it, a bottle of distilled water, several bottle cleaners, and way in the bottom, a sheet of paper. I slowly freed the sheet and glanced down at what was a birth certificate, but the mother's name was blacked out. "Her name is Dixie Summer Witter. She's about six months old, give or take a week."

He snatched the paper from my hands with an apologetic smile before he gave the document his full attention.

I watched in twisted fascination as at least a dozen different emotions splashed across his face. There was so much happening behind those green eyes, and I was more curious than I should be about the details. Suddenly, every emotion melted away and left a blank stare in its place. He lifted his gaze to meet mine, something akin to embarrassment in his eyes.

"I hate to do this so soon, but, ah, do you think you'll be all right on your own for a couple of hours? I need to talk to my agent immediately."

Agent. That was a big clue about what kind of big shot Mr. Witter was. "Sure." I frowned because I couldn't conjure up an image of him in anything I've seen recently. "You're an actor?"

Mr. Witter unleashed a beaming smile that made it clear why he was a Hollywood heartthrob here in Texas. "No. I'm a hockey player."

Okay, now I was really confused. "There's hockey in Houston?"

Mr. Witter's smile faded and I worried, for a moment, that I might have offended him. But a beat later, a loud laugh exploded out of him, startling both me and Dixie. "I promise to be offended by that later, but for now, I really need to head out."

"Dixie and I will be fine for a couple of hours, but this isn't enough to even get us through the night." I patted the daisy diaper bag on the sofa to remind him that this wasn't something we could postpone.

"Yeah, okay," he nodded absently, clearly distracted. "This first and then baby supplies." He slipped into a pair of sneakers and grabbed his keyes.

"Uh, Mr. Witter?"

He stopped and studied me. "Call me, Alex. You'll be living in my home, no need to be so formal."

"Okay then, Alex. You might want to put on a shirt before you head out."

He looked down at his sculpted bare chest and grinned. "Good idea. Thank you, Sasha. You're already helping." He disappeared down the hall and returned a few minutes later in a fresh pair of jeans and a black t-shirt, looking like a big, beautiful, blond Viking before he rushed out of the apartment.

I turned to Dixie who was still studying my face with a ghost of a smile on her lips. "It's just you and me for a while, kiddo. Let's get to know each other." I held her close and got acquainted with my new work and living space.

Chapter 5

Alex

Jack's brown eyes held mine for a long, silent moment. With his elbows resting on his desk and his hands steepled together, he watched me until the silence became uncomfortable. Maddeningly uncomfortable.

"What the hell did you do?"

My brows knitted into a scowl. "Why do you assume I did anything?"

"Oh please," Jack scoffed. "You show up at my office willingly and without an appointment? You did something and you think showing up here will soften the blow. So, hit me with it."

Sometimes I hated that he knew me so well, and worse that I knew him too. I'd known Jack well enough to know that he wasn't going to react well, which yeah, was exactly why I'd shown up unannounced.

"I have a baby." The words kind of tumbled out of my

mouth because I just needed to get them out before I said anything else.

"Explain."

I nodded as I inhaled deeply and let it out slowly, repeating the move five times until I knew I could tell him everything I knew without stopping. "I can do the math to narrow down who the mother could be, and I'd like to do that, but my first priority is a DNA test."

"The first intelligent thing you've said." Jack scribbled on the ever-present legal pad in front of him. "You'll need someone to care for the child when training starts."

I flashed a proud smile, finally relaxed enough to drop down in the black leather chair directly across from Jack. "Already did that."

"You did? She needs to be a professional, not some woman trying to become Mrs. Witter, Alex."

"No shit. Give me a little bit of credit. I went to the service Dante used and I have a nanny. Her name is Sasha, and the best part? She has no fucking clue who I am." I recounted her disbelief at the fact that there was a hockey team in Texas. "It was a small blow to my ego but the relief overrode it."

"That's good. I'll have NDAs drawn up for the nanny and the woman who runs the business. In the meantime, you need to keep the child under wraps. Don't take her out with you in public, and for the love of money, do not let anyone get a picture of you and the child together."

"Dixie," I grunted protectively. "Her name is Dixie. Not *the child*." Why I suddenly felt so protective, I couldn't say, but Jack's attitude rubbed me the wrong way. "And she's a baby, she needs fresh air and sunlight."

Jack barked out a laugh, his expression was a mixture of annoyance and disbelief. "She's a baby, Alex, not a fucking house plant. If she needs fresh air and sun, take her on the roof." He rolled his eyes as if that was a reasonable solution.

"I'll make sure Sasha takes her out alone so we're not photographed together," I promised him in the spirit of compromise. "I need a discreet and fast DNA test, and then I want someone to find where the mother is without contacting her." I produced the birth certificate and handed it to Jack, watching as his eyes bounced over all the pertinent details.

"You don't need to do the math, Alex. Her name is right here on the birth certificate."

"Duh," I acknowledged. "But unless you can read through permanent marker, we still don't have an answer." I shook my head. "There's just one name visible and I don't recall any woman named Julie. "It's always Tatiana or Veronica, Selena or Veronika. Something exotic, not normal."

Jack stared at me with his mouth wide open. "You sound like an asshole, you know that right?"

I shrugged. "I'm being honest. There hasn't been a Julie or a Marie."

My agent leaned forward, gaze narrowed on mine. "No Julia or Maria," he asked with different accents.

"No." I spent much of the ride to Jack's downtown

offices trying to piece together who I'd been with fifteen months ago. "That was a long time ago and there have been a lot of women since." Not my best argument, but it was all I had. The truth.

"I'll get an investigator on it, don't worry. What I need you to worry about Alex, is keeping the existence of the child under wraps at least until we have the paternity results." He noticed my reaction and held up his hands in a defensive gesture. "We need to be certain she's yours before we figure out our next move, unless you don't mind walking away from millions of dollars?"

"You know damn well I don't."

"Then listen to me for once in your life."

"You haven't steered me wrong yet. Except for that underwear ad." I smiled and Jack barked out a laugh.

"That ad made you a household name and it's why we're both so wealthy today."

Yeah, I couldn't deny that, but it wasn't exactly discreet, being on twenty foot tall billboards in nothing but my underwear. "All right, then. I need to get back to the penthouse."

"Go," he said and shooed me out of his office. "And keep your dick away from the nanny."

I laughed off his words, but as the elevator took me down to the underground parking, I thought about the nanny. Sasha. She was a beautiful woman with her thick black hair that hung down her back in soft waves and big blue eyes that always appeared to be laughing. Don't even get me started on those killer curves. She was more than a foot shorter than my six-foot-six-inch frame, and she wore those curves like a fucking badge of honor, not hiding behind loose fitting clothes like too many curvy women did.

She's off-limits, I reminded myself as I entered the penthouse, noting immediately that it was too quiet. Dixie was a baby chatterbox, unless she was eating or sleeping, she cooed and babbled nonstop, but now there was nothing. With a frown, I went through the penthouse.

"Sasha? Dixie?" I couldn't find them anywhere and panic settled in, where in the hell were they?

The door that led to the roof hung open just a few inches and I yanked it all the way open and took the stairs two at a time. A soft, melodic sound met my ears before I made it to the roof and I stopped at the top at the sight of Sasha with Dixie in her arms, head resting on her shoulders as she walked around the rooftop singing softly to her.

Sasha spotted me and flashed a sweet smile. "Everything okay, Alex?"

"I'm not sure," I admitted easily, maybe too easily, as I drew closer to woman and child. "Everything is in the works, which I guess means it's on its way to being okay."

"Every solution starts with a plan so you're on your way." Her blue eyes studied me for a minute and I wondered what she saw. She didn't know who I was, so what she thought of me was anybody's guess. "I picked out rooms for me and Dixie. The adjoining suites at the other end of the hall so I can get to her easily at night without disturbing you, or when you're around. I assume hockey has away games?"

I laughed at her question. "Yeah, about half the season is away, which is something else I need to think about. For now, we have baby supplies to worry about. You said something about a changing table?"

She nodded and reached into her back pocket for her phone, pressing her cheek to the top of Dixie's head in an unconscious gesture of affection. "I made you a list." She swiped the screen and handed me the phone. "I know it's going to cost a lot and we can do some comparison shopping for much of it, but it is all necessary. I promise."

I smiled again. She mistook my shocked silence as an objection to the potential price tag. "It's not the cost. It just seems like a lot of stuff for such a little thing."

Unlike her sweet voice, her laugh was throaty and low, and perfectly matched her curves. "Babies need a lot of stuff."

This list was as large as the one the decorator had given me to furnish this whole damn penthouse, but what did I know about babies? "We can get a lot of this online, can't we?"

"We can," she agreed. "But even if it all arrives tomorrow morning, there are necessities like diapers and formula that we'll run out of before then."

Indecision weighed heavily on my chest and I knew I would have to be straight with Sasha about my situation.

"Look, I can pop out and grab a few things to get us through the night." Her lips pulled into a phoney smile at my obvious relief at her offer. "But you should probably give me cash."

I froze at her words, wondering if I could trust this woman.

Sasha let out a sigh of frustration as she rested one hand on Dixie's back. "I Googled you while you were gone and I'm guessing that a strange woman buying baby items with your credit card might end up splashed on the headlines tomorrow."

"Yeah," I agreed easily, already imagining what Jack would have to say about that. But another, more pressing thought occurred to me. What if Sasha didn't return with what I needed? What if she took the money and ran, and then sold the story to the tabloids? I couldn't risk that.

"Alex," she growled but managed to keep her voice low so as not to wake Dixie. "You hired me. You asked for me specifically, and I'm trustworthy. If you can't trust me with a few thousand dollars then you shouldn't trust me with your kid."

She was right, of course. Then again, wouldn't a scam artist have all the answers to get me to trust her?

Another sigh of frustration escaped from Sasha as she plucked her phone from my hands. "Fine. I'll send you the list and you can go get the items yourself. Just give me your phone number, or is that too personal as well?" Without waiting for an answer, she started towards the door. "I'll write the list on a piece of paper and you can get what you think she needs until tomorrow."

I hurried behind Sasha, willing my gaze to stay off the

small dip of her waist before her swaying hips came into view, and her round ass.

Stop it, Alex. Stop that shit right now.

"Sasha," I called after her but she was on a roll and when I found her inside the penthouse she had Dixie settled into her carrier and was bent over a sheet of paper, writing faster than I'd ever seen anyone write. "Sasha, stop."

The stubborn woman didn't stop, though. She continued to scribble on the paper until she was done, at which point she pressed the paper against my chest. "There. Happy shopping." She flashed a wide grin that was sassy and just a small bit devious.

"You're going to be a handful, aren't you?"

"Me?" She put a hand to her chest and did her best to look innocent. "I'm just trying to help, Alex."

I shook my head and reached in my pocket for my wallet. "Okay, you win Sasha," I told her as I fished a few hundred dollar bills from the wallet. "This should be enough to get us started. Get whatever you can and we'll shop for the rest together online. Deal?"

She stared wide-eyed at the stack of cash on the counter. "That seems like too much."

I frowned. "You said a few thousand."

"It's called hyperbole," she shot back, her gaze darted between me and the cash.

"I don't know how much a changing table costs. Or even diapers. Take it and get everything you can with it." Another thought occurred to me. "Do you have a car?"

"Yes."

"Okay. That's good. Get what'll fit in your car and Barry will help you when you return." I slid my phone across the counter. "We need to be able to contact each other."

Her shoulders relaxed. "If you're sure?"

"I am. This is all new to me so this probably won't be the last time I piss you off." I flashed what I hoped was a charming smile.

"Duly noted," she replied with the barest hint of a smile. "As long as you know that pretty smile won't stop me from calling you out when it's necessary."

My smile grew brighter at her words. "I expect nothing less."

She gave a sharp nod and scanned the room until she found her purse, shoved the money inside and slipped out the door.

It doesn't matter how hot and sassy she is. She's the nanny and I'm staying out of trouble. That's what I told myself but I had a feeling that once again, trouble would find me.

Chapter 6

Sasha

With the money Alex gave me to shop for baby necessities I could have gone shopping in any of the luxury boutiques that lined the small streets, or stopped at River Oaks. Dixie would have everything she needed, only with a big price tag. Instead, I drove a little past the boutiques and luxury vehicles and stopped at one of those big box baby stores. I'd be able to get more of what she needed for the same money, plus a few extras.

And since I was here on my own, I didn't need to ask anyone's permission. Forgiveness? Maybe, but that was a worry for another time. For now, I grabbed the biggest shopping cart they had and picked up one of those hand-held devices that would allow me to scan the bigger items without hauling them around the store.

It was odd, doing this kind of shopping on my own, like I was someone's mother picking up necessities to make my life easier. Technically all of that was true, except the part where I was Dixie's mother. It was good practice anyway, just in case one day I actually had kids, and a family of my own. This job wasn't conducive to a successful relationship, which meant someday I would have to choose between my career and my future. It wasn't as easy a decision as some might think, giving up that independence and becoming wholly reliant on someone else for your survival.

I couldn't bring myself to do that, not again. Not ever again.

Maudlin thoughts, much?

I shrugged off those thoughts and added more bottles and nipples to the cart, more bottle cleaners, four triple packs of baby wipes along with a month's worth of onesies. It was enough to get us through the week, and then Alex could take care of the rest. Okay, and I might have added a few pink and yellow dresses to the cart, and the most adorable pair of baby sandals I'd ever seen. Maybe it was overkill, but there was no such thing when it came to a little girl without a mother as far as I was concerned.

My phone rang as I turned into the aisle holding all the diaper bins, and though I knew I would regret answering the call, I did.

"Hello, Mom." It wasn't that I didn't love my mother, because I did. She was just a lot to deal with most of the time.

"Sasha. I'm surprised you answered." No one did the tone that was a mix of hurt and disappointment as well as my mother. "Does this mean you're making time to come back for a visit?" The hope in her words almost made me reconsider, but the truth was the truth.

"Sorry, Mom. I can't. I've just accepted another placement, which means it'll be at least a few more months before I can even think of coming for a visit." The truth was whenever I thought about returning home, the answer came quickly and decisively. Hell no.

Mom let out what I liked to call the *disappointed mother's sigh* and I could almost picture her pinching the bridge of her nose as if I was the source of all of her troubles.

"You will have to forgive him at some point, Sasha. He's your father."

I rolled my eyes. "It would have been nice if he'd remembered that over the years," I shot back. "And for the record, I don't have to forgive him. Not if I don't want to. But it's irrelevant right now because he isn't the reason I can't come home." The fact that my mother stayed with my father after all the abuse and the affairs didn't do much to encourage visits back to Connecticut. "I have to work, Mom. That's how the bills get paid and how I take care of myself."

Not that I had very many expenses here in Texas. Usually, I stayed with one of the other girls between assignments, but I'd been with Jenna and James for just over five years so it's been a while since I've had to pay rent or utilities. It was another benefit of having a live-in position.

"You shouldn't have to work just to survive, Sasha."

I rolled my eyes as I scanned the best rated diaper disposal system and added it to the tally. "You mean like ninety percent of the rest of the world does?"

"Exactly. You're too smart and too privileged to work like a commoner."

I bit back the smart ass comment that was on the tip of my tongue and sighed instead. I decided that a drastic, unsubtle change of topic was my best bet for not ending this conversation in a shouting match with my mother.

"Anyway, how are you doing Mom?" I walked up and down the aisles as I listened to Mom drone on about her friends at the country club, the many committees she sat on, not to mention the latest charity gala she was helping to plan. It was the mundane details of her life that made me miss my mother fiercely, just not enough to come back to Connecticut.

Not enough to see *him*.

"Oh, Sasha, you remember Wallace Emerson? He's back in town and I have to admit that he's had what you kids call a *glow-up*. Now he is both handsome and accomplished with his shiny new MBA."

"Good for Wallace." He was, of course, a douchebag of the highest order, and that was being as kind as I was prepared to be when it came to him. "I'm glad to hear you're keeping busy."

Mom groaned to show her frustration, something she only did with me. "Wallace would make a good husband."

"For some woman maybe, but even that's doubtful." I

would rather stay single before entering into a loveless marriage or worse, a dangerous one. "Are you in charge of planning the Emerald Ball again this year?" It was the perfect topic to distract her from trying to marry me off to one of her friend's awful sons. Her entire life was this ball or that gala, raising money for a worthwhile cause, but mostly just for show.

"Sasha, please," she begged while I'd spaced out on our conversation. "You can't be a nanny forever and Wallace is a good man from a good family."

I laughed, the sound was harsh and bitter. "As if you would know what a good man looks like. Wallace will be just like his father and mine, drunk and abusive and disrespectful." I knew the words were a mistake before they flew from my mouth, but it was too late to take them back, not that I would even if I could. I knew the truth about my family and their peers, and I was the only one who dared to voice that truth out loud.

"I guess you just know everything there is to know about everything, don't you?"

"No, Mom. I never said that. I don't know everything, and neither do you, but you insist on trying to dictate how I live my life even though I've told you so many times that I don't want *your* life. Why can't you just let it go?"

"I just want you to be happy, sweetheart."

I sighed, knowing there was no point in saying what I was about to say next. "I just want you to be happy too, Mom. That's the one thing we can agree on. While I am grateful for the opportunities your life has given me, I don't want to live like that."

"Because it was so awful?"

"Mom," I sighed knowing my patience would snap soon. "Yeah, it was pretty awful, not knowing what kind of mood he'd be in after a long day at work. Locking my door so he wouldn't wake me up with a lashing. Hearing you scream for your life. Awful is putting it mildly."

"Everyone makes mistakes, Sasha."

"Yes, they do. But it's only a mistake if they don't repeat them, and if they're sorry." My father was neither. He was defiant about his past deeds. "I miss you, Mom. But I'm done having this conversation. Love you. Goodbye," I murmured and ended the call before she could rope me into another conversation that went nowhere.

I stared at the picture of my mother, smiling shyly as I snapped a photo of her when I last saw her, eighteen months ago. I stared with a heavy heart until the screen turned black. And then, with my mood soured, I finished shopping and paid for everything as two young workers helped me load everything into my SUV.

I stopped at my favorite sandwich shop and bought the biggest, sloppiest hoagie I could, plus one for Alex, and made my way back to my temporary home.

Chapter 7

Alex

I woke up the next morning with a start, my heart racing as I looked around my bedroom and paused. I didn't hear Dixie crying which at first filled me with relief and then concern. I jumped out of bed and yanked open my bedroom door as I tried to clear the fog of sleep from my brain. The scent of bacon hit me first, and in the next moment, dread washed over me when I realized that I hadn't reached out to my chef or housekeeper, or any of the other weekly staff who made my life easier to let them know there had been changes.

"Dammit." Instead of stopping at the room at the other end of the hall to check on Dixie and Sasha, I went to the kitchen, hoping I could have a quick chat with Henrietta before she put the pieces together on her own. I bit out a curse under my breath as I stopped in the middle of the kitchen and stared at the scene before me. Sasha was dressed in jeans and a tank top, yet somehow she still looked sinfully delicious, while Henrietta jostled a giggling Dixie in her arms.

"Good morning." Sasha flashed a quick smile and turned back to the stove.

"Mornin'," I growled and turned my attention to my housekeeper who smiled up at me with one salt and pepper brow arched knowingly.

"Seems to be a lot of changes going on around here, Alex."

Henrietta had been with me since I moved to Houston about six years ago, and there was genuine affection between us, which meant lying to her wasn't easy.

"I didn't know where to start. Or what to say," I admitted sheepishly.

Sasha flashed a compassionate smile in my direction. "I made it easy for you. This is Dixie and I'm her nanny," she explained, holding my gaze in a moment of silent communication, which I somehow understood, and then she turned away again.

Wait one damned minute, when did I start silently communicating with my nanny? I didn't know, and I didn't have the mental bandwidth to handle it this early in the morning.

"That about covers it."

"Coffee pot is full," Sasha added cheerfully.

I nodded and grunted my gratitude as I headed across the kitchen to the coffeepot. The doorbell rang and I froze.

"I'll get it," Henrietta offered. "She's just too cute, Alex. Well done." With those words, Henrietta placed

Dixie into her highchair, pinched her chubby cheek and shuffled off towards the front door.

"You didn't have to step in for me like that," I told Sasha as I savored the first few gulps of black coffee.

"I didn't *step in*," she shot back. "I simply introduced myself and then Dixie to your housekeeper who was mighty surprised to find us both here when she arrived."

"You're upset."

"I'm not," she said even as she dumped a skillet full of scrambled eggs onto a large platter. "I'm merely explaining what I did and why."

"Jack is here," Henrietta grumbled, just in case there was any confusion about her feelings about my agent. "And he brought a friend."

Jack greeted me with a handshake and nodded to the man in the blue suit. "Dr. Peterson is here to do the DNA swabs." His gaze settled on Sasha first and his blond brows shot up behind his hair in surprise before he shot a thunderous expression my way. Remembering his manners, Jack stepped forward and introduced himself to Sasha.

"I'm Jack Gentry, Alex's agent."

"I'm Sasha, the nanny, though I'm sure you know that. Hungry?"

He flashed a smile of surprise and nodded. "I could eat." He glanced over his shoulder with another surprised expression and I nodded because I understood.

She was a wonder, full of both sass and warmth. Not to mention stunning.

"Where should we do this, Doc?"

"Anywhere with a flat surface is acceptable. I'll need you and the child."

"I'll come with you," Henrietta offered and scooped Dixie from her highchair and kissed her cheek. "Let's go little one. It'll be quick and painless, I'm sure."

I hoped she was right. I led the doctor to a corner in the living room and waited impatiently as he wrote on glass tubes and slipped gloves on his fingers. "Okay, Mr. Witter, have you ever done this before?"

"No."

Dr. Peterson nodded. "This is a quick buccal swab." He stuck a giant cotton swab in my mouth and swiped at the inside of my cheek, and then did the same to Dixie.

I relaxed and listened carefully as he explained the process and what to expect. "When will we have the results?"

"Two days maximum. Call with this identification code and you'll have the results. Or you can pick them up if you need the paper."

"Perfect. Thank you, Doctor." We all returned to the kitchen where Jack was eating and Sasha sat across from him looking over the boilerplate non-disclosure agreement.

"What about other employees at Elite Nanny Service,?" She asked sincerely.

Jack arched a brow. "Eager to gossip with the other nannies?"

I took a step forward ready to tell Jack to back off, but Sasha didn't need me to rush to her defense. She hit my agent with a searing gaze.

"No. I'm used to working for rich people, but not famous people. A few of the other nannies have though, and if I need guidance or advice, I'd like to be able to get it. Unless you moonlighted as a child care professional in college, Jack?"

Henrietta snorted a laugh.

"No, I have no nanny skills, unfortunately. But I have spoken to Serenity, and she assures me you all sign NDAs when you start with a new household so you should be fine, just don't give away intimate details."

Her gaze was alight with amusement as she glanced at me and then back at Jack. "Don't worry, I won't tell anyone he sleeps in fancy pin-striped boxer briefs."

I looked down at her words and for the first time since I was a kid, I felt a blush rise up my body. How in the hell had so much happened before I even managed to get dressed for the day?

"I, um, guess I should get dressed."

"Good idea," Jack said before he barked out a laugh at my expense.

When I returned in a pair of jeans and a t-shirt, Dr. Peterson was leaving with a breakfast sandwich in his hand and Sasha had finally sat down to eat, taking the spot beside Dixie who was fascinated by a yellow strip of something.

"What is that?"

"It's an omelet with salt, garlic, and herbs. Dixie is about the age where she should be starting solid foods so I thought I'd see where she was with that."

Sure enough, Dixie grabbed the small rectangular piece and shoved it in her mouth, chewing contemplatively. "How did you know?"

"Education and experience," she shot back and then gave Dixie and her breakfast, her full attention.

"Not bad," Jack whispered, referring to Sasha. "Her boss signed an NDA and the investigator is looking for the mother. You sure you don't want me to handle it?"

"No. At least not until I know everything." Jack was a pit bull, it was what made him such a great agent, but not every situation needed his particular skillset.

Jack finished his breakfast and got up from the table. "Then my work here is done. We'll talk soon, Alex. In the meantime, try to stay out of trouble."

I nodded at the familiar refrain and once he was gone, I dug into my own now lukewarm breakfast. So far the day was off to a good start. It wasn't how I usually started my day—with a workout, a few calls and some time on the ice—but this was controlled chaos, and for today, that was a win.

Chapter 8

Sasha

With Dixie asleep in her new crib, I decided to take advantage of the peace and quiet, using the time to put away the three big baskets of freshly laundered baby clothes. This little girl already had more clothes than I did, and sure, it was mostly my fault for buying so many adorable outfits for her, but it was only as I stuffed the closet and the tiny armoire that I realized my indulgence.

An hour later, all the clothes had a place to call home, so did the toys and even the necessities like diapers and wipes. Dixie's room was in perfect order and I looked around the room with a satisfied smile before grabbing the monitor and making my way towards the kitchen for a glass of water.

I drank down a full glass of cold water and refilled it immediately, letting the icy liquid cool my overheated body. Though the penthouse was very well air conditioned, I felt warm enough that I already removed the cardigan I had on earlier. It was common in Texas. Sometimes even a steady blast of cold air was no match for the Texas heat.

It had been a busy day already with Alex's agent showing up with a doctor to do swabs for paternity testing. I couldn't help but smile as I thought about Alex's face when he realized he'd been running around in his underwear all morning. Then again, a body like his was worth showing off, from a strictly objective point of view. He was gorgeous and fit, that wasn't in question.

Keep telling yourself that, sister.

Yeah, okay. If I was being honest with myself I could admit—only to myself—that Alex was a knockout. He was classically handsome with thick blond hair and sparkling green eyes that glittered when he smiled. And his body? Well it was the stuff of every woman's X-rated fantasies.

"Excuse me."

Alex's deep voice startled a yelp out of me, which was bad enough, but my body jerked, sending all the water in my glass up in the air before it promptly landed on my head, and his bare chest.

"Holy hell, man. You scared me." Eventually I managed to tear my gaze away from his bronzed, muscled chest and look up at his smirking face.

"Sorry?" He shrugged and reached across my body, his heavily corded forearm brushed across my stomach as he reached for a bottle of water in the fridge. "I thought you heard me."

I took a few steps back and rolled my eyes. "Well maybe if you didn't walk around like a ninja, I would have heard you."

Alex barked out a laugh and shook his head. "You're the first person to ever say that. I'm only graceful and stealthy on the ice."

"Obviously none of those people have ever lived with you."

"They wish," he answered with a smile before he turned the bottle upside down and finished it in just a few seconds. His gaze settled on mine, his expression suddenly serious. "I should apologize for Jack. He can be a little over the top at times."

Jack was exactly what I expected of a man who looked out for tough guys like Alex. "Don't apologize. It's good that you have people in your life looking out for you." It was more than I had in my life, so who was I to judge?

"Yeah well, he could look out for me without being so overbearing about it." Alex's laugh told me there was genuine affection between the men, which only made me more curious about their relationship. "I ordered everything you left in the shopping cart," he said, changing the subject. "It should all arrive tomorrow morning."

My eyes rounded in shock. "You bought it all?"

His brows dipped in confusion. "Yeah. You said she needed it all, right?"

I nodded, words escaping me for a minute. I didn't

know how to ask the question that formed on the tip of my tongue in a nice way. "But what if, ugh, never mind."

"What if she's not mine." It wasn't a question because clearly, it was on his mind too. Alex's broad shoulders shrugged. "If she's not, then she'll go wherever she's going in style."

His words surprised me and caused a pinch in my chest, not because his words were sweet and kind, okay not *just* because they were sweet and kind, but because it meant Dixie's young life would be filled with upheaval and uncertainty.

"That's nice of you."

"What can I say? I'm a nice guy."

"So far, I have to agree." I started to relax, well as much as I could with him standing in front of me showing off steel-cut abs and bulging pecs, and I even managed a smile. "How are you doing with all of this, really?"

A sigh of what looked like relief escaped, and Alex put his hands on his hips, his green gaze studying me closely almost as if he was trying to decide whether or not to trust me with his feelings.

"I have no fucking clue, Sasha. I mean one minute I was enjoying a solo dinner of steak and beer and the next there was a little girl with my eyes clinging to me for dear life. How am I supposed to feel?"

It was a lot to deal with for anyone, but especially for a guy like Alex who'd been living a mostly carefree life. "You're supposed to feel however you feel. Are you angry?

Scared? Whatever you're feeling, own it so you can deal with it."

"Just like that, huh?"

"Yeah, that's the abridged version of course, without all the steps of owning it and dealing with it." There were plenty of issues in my own life that required those same steps so I knew the work needed to deal with it. "It's a process."

His smile came slowly. "That's the catch, then?"

I nodded. "There's always a catch. You can be a superstar hockey player without the press invading your every waking moment."

He growled his disapproval at my words. "No kidding. Now I'll have both you and Jack on my case." Once again his gaze studied me and I resisted the urge to squirm under his appraisal. "What about you, Sasha?"

I blinked and then frowned. "What about me?"

"Where are you from? How did you get into the nanny biz?" He shrugged and slid between me and the fridge, in search of food, no doubt.

I hated talking about my past, but it had been so long since someone actually asked about it, that the words tumbled out easily. "I'm from Connecticut, born and raised there until I left for college."

"Where did you go to college?"

Okay, so we're really doing this. I sighed as I answered. "Undergrad in Chicago and graduate school in California."

"Wow. Smart. Your folks must be proud as hell of you."

I laughed bitterly at his words. "I can assure you that they're not proud. They would be proud if I married the right man, which means a man from the right family with a *good* name." I shook off the thoughts of the last conversation with my mother. "Anyway I received my degrees in early childhood development and education and child psychology and I wasn't exactly sure what to do with it. While I was trying to figure it out and dodge my parents, Serenity found me and I ended up here."

Alex let out a long, low whistle. "So you're still deciding, then?"

"No," I sighed. "I've decided. Turns out my experience combined with my education has made me a good nanny." I didn't want him to ask why, so I turned the tables. "How did you become a hockey player?"

He laughed as he stepped back from the fridge with an arm full of sandwich ingredients, talking as he assembled them. "It might surprise you to learn there aren't a lot of hockey opportunities in the backwoods of Tennessee."

I grinned. "I thought I heard a hint of a southern accent in there."

He flashed a proud smile. "Crayfish Hills," he admitted with a shy grin. "I had a bit of a temper as a kid and I had exactly one friend who came from a so-called normal family. His dad noticed my temper and suggested hockey as a way to deal with it. My family couldn't afford the equipment, never mind the team expense for me to play, so Mr. Morris paid for it and he taught me to play. Early in the morning and on the weekends, sometimes evenings after school. Turns out, I had a head for the game. It was the first time anyone had ever done something like that for me and it meant something. It meant a lot, actually."

Ah, hell. His sincere words combined with that look on his face started the unfortunate stirrings of a crush. "That's sweet."

His green gaze narrowed in my direction but I just laughed. "I was recruited to a fancy private school for high school to play, and then college, going early in the draft."

"A real Cinderella story. Good for you." It was nice to see that everything he had was borne of hard work and determination, rather than his name or upbringing. "Do you enjoy it?"

"I do. It was the best thing that ever happened to me."

I stared at the strange mix of the man who was big and tough, working in a brutal profession, but also managed honesty and sincerity with ease.

"Will Dixie put a kink in your social life?"

He laughed. "You really haven't looked me up online?"

I sighed as I shook my head. "Just briefly. I probably should have done a deep dive, but I know better than most just how little you can believe what is written about the rich and famous. Plus, everything moved so fast with this placement, I spent all of last two days settling Dixie."

Curiosity burned in his gaze as he put the finishing

touches on the biggest sandwich I'd ever seen, but he didn't ask. "She might slow me down but that's not necessarily a bad thing. After my brief relationship with Tatiana went south, she decided to share intimate details of our time together with the world."

My eyes bulged out of my head in shock. "Tatiana? You dated her? She's gorgeous!" She was tall and leggy and busty, the absolute trifecta where most men were concerned.

"She's gorgeous," he agreed. "But that's all she is. Trust me." The look of disgust on his face urged me to believe him.

"Well I know a thing or two about that. Not beauty, per se, but it's all about appearances in my world, or rather my parents' small world. *But he's from a good family. Don't you know who his great-grandfather was?*" I scoffed and rolled my eyes. "As if any of that says a damn thing about the person or their character."

His eyes grew wide and his mouth dropped open. "You're a rich girl."

My face burned with embarrassment and I shook my head. "I'm not. My parents are rich and I grew up that way, but I'm a nanny." Technically all of that was true. I had a substantial trust fund, but I didn't use it so I wasn't really rich. Right?

"We're a fine pair, aren't we? You're a rich girl playing at being poor and I'm a poor kid pretending like I belong."

I laughed. "Something tells me that you've always belonged, Alex. You just didn't realize it."

He flashed a satisfied smile and took a huge bite of his sandwich. "Thanks."

I shook my head when he offered me a bite of the monstrous sandwich. "No thanks." But I did have another question that was as much for my sake as for Dixie's. "What do you plan to do about Dixie?"

He shrugged and finished chewing. "Not sure. Well, that's a lie. If she's mine then she's my kid, my blood and I will do everything in my power to give her the best life possible. I'll make sure she's protected and cared for. Period."

Good. "That's what every little kid needs."

"I agree." His jaw was tense and I had a feeling that although our backgrounds were worlds apart, our experiences weren't.

"And if she's not yours?"

He shrugged again. "I don't even want to think about it, Sasha. I don't know what I want the test results to say, which makes me an asshole, doesn't it?"

"No. It's okay to have complicated feelings on this. You thought your life was going to look one way and now that's changed. You'll have the results soon enough and then you can figure out what your new life is going to look like."

He frowned. "This is one of those things where all the spaces between the words require a lot of damn work, isn't it?"

I nodded. "Now you're getting it." Dixie started to fuss on the monitor and I picked it up, attached it to my back pocket, and started for the baby's room. "Good luck."

"Yeah, thanks," he grumbled to my back.

I wanted to laugh at his put-out tone but I refused to let myself laugh or smile. I could not, would not allow myself to crush on the hockey player or the sexy single dad. Or my boss.

Nope. Now way. No how.

Absolutely not.

Chapter 9

Alex

"That can't be possible." The words squeezed out through my clenched jaws as I tried to keep my anger at bay. "I placed the order and it was processed. My credit card was charged including the exorbitant delivery fees, which means you're responsible for bringing all the items to the address I provided."

"I'm sorry about the mix-up, sir."

"It isn't a mix-up," I growled. "It is a total failure on your end."

The customer service rep had the nerve to sigh as if I was causing her a big fat fucking headache. "Deliveries are scheduled and you are not on the schedule for today, but you are more than welcome to pick the items up at the store." She rattled off the address as if that was a perfectly reasonable compromise.

"No!" I barked into the phone. "If you can't make the delivery in the next hour, I expect a full refund today."

"But, sir," she began and I cut her off.

"Can you make that happen?"

There was a long silence before she sighed. "No. The delivery drivers have their schedules for the day, but we can have the order ready for pickup so all you have to do is pull up and our guys will load you up."

It was a tempting option even if it wasn't ideal. "Fine," I growled eventually and ended the call.

"Everything okay?" Sasha's soft voice had a calming effect that left me slightly unnerved but I focused on the calming part for now because I needed it.

"No." I explained about the delivery fuck up, failing miserably to keep my anger out of my voice. "So now I have to pick it up or wait until tomorrow."

"Don't you have an assistant or something who does stuff like this for you?"

I frowned. "Why would I need an assistant when they were supposed to deliver it?"

She shrugged. "Don't give me attitude, I didn't screw up the order. And don't people like you always have assistants?"

"Now you sound like Jack," I growled. He'd been tossing assistants my way for years but I always refused. "I am perfectly capable of taking care of myself. Mostly." I grinned and she rolled her eyes. "The point is, they were supposed to deliver it and they messed up."

"Cool, so you can be mad about it or you can fix it. Which are you going to do?"

My first instinct was to frown, because no one, especially women, ever spoke to me like that. But as her words sank in, my anger slowly dissolved. She was right.

"I guess I'm going to pick up the stuff. Want to come along?"

She frowned. "I'm pretty sure Jack said that you were not to appear in public with Dixie."

I shrugged. "We won't technically be in public. You and Dixie will be in the car while I oversee the guys loading up the truck. No one will even see you."

She looked indecisive, and I should have just let it go at that, but for reasons I didn't want to explore, I couldn't.

"Okay. Let me get Dixie ready and we can head out."

"It's not funny," I growled twenty minutes later as Sasha watched me, laughing as I struggled to get the damn car seat installed.

"You're right," she sighed and handed Dixie to me. "It's hilarious. Watch closely," she said as she slid the seatbelt through the base easily, as if she created the wretched thing herself. She took the seat from me and held it up. "Listen for the snap," she said as she shoved the seat onto the base, and a loud snap sounded. "And she's safe and secure." Her proud smile took the sting off the fact that she was able to do it easily.

"Yeah, sure."

She laughed, the sound sexy and lyrical as she rested a hand on my shoulder. "It takes some practice, that's all. But you will have to learn it eventually."

I appreciated that Sasha didn't rub it in or admonish me for my inability to do something so simple. Her words of encouragement with that hint of challenge was just what I needed to hear. "You would be a damn good coach."

"A hockey coach?" She frowned in the passenger seat. "All I know about hockey is you put the black thingy into the net."

"That *thingy* is a puck, and not necessarily hockey but anything. Tennis coach. Life coach. Figure skating coach. You've perfected tough love without being an asshole about it."

"Thanks," she laughed. "I think."

We pulled up to the pickup station and I left Sasha and Dixie in the car, finally calm after the company's earlier mistake. Five minutes later, my expression was thunderous as I stomped back to the car. "The entire order is wrong."

Sasha frowned. "It'll be faster together, but I think you should stay in the car while Dixie and I do the shopping."

"I can't ask you to do that again."

"You're not asking, I'm volunteering. Do you have a better plan?"

"You know I don't."

"Then you stay here and I'll rush through the store and scan everything again. Let's hope this time it works."

She was right. Of course, she was right. "Fine." I watched the swing of her hips as she moved to the store's entrance, angry that Jack had put these restraints on me. *Don't do it,* my conscience warned after about fifteen minutes of sitting in the car and doing nothing.

At the twenty-minute mark, I went inside and found Sasha chatting with Dixie who smiled and babbled as if she understood.

"What can I do?"

Sasha let out a shocked gasp and turned, punching my shoulder before she could stop herself. "Sorry, but stop sneaking up on me!"

I smiled and rubbed the spot she'd hit. "Nice jab."

"Thanks. Self-defense classes." She turned back to Dixie and pushed the cart forward. "What're you doing here?"

"Helping."

"This is a bad idea," she said in a sing-song voice meant for Dixie. "But he's gonna do what he's gonna do, am I right?"

Dixie's smile grew and she responded with a loud series of shrieks and gargles.

"See? Even Dixie knows." Her playful smile made me relax as we went up and down the aisles, replacing every single item that had been in the shopping cart just last night.

Being with Sasha was easy. She was funny and easy to talk to, and she wasn't at all in awe of me for being a celebrity.

"No one even notices me," I assured her when she spotted two young women staring in our direction. "They just see a good-looking man."

She laughed. "Or maybe they see a very *familiar* good-looking man."

"Then they would come and ask for a photo or an autograph," I told her honestly. Fans were never shy about approaching and asking for what they wanted, no matter how ill-timed their appearance might be. But it was because of the fans I got paid so well to do something I loved.

"Do you ever go out, like, incognito? With a wig and a big nose and sunglasses?"

I laughed. "No. Given my size, it's difficult to hide who I am most of the time." Sometimes I was confused for a football player or a superhero, but people always assumed I was *somebody* they knew. Dixie began to fuss and instinctively, I unfastened her and held her close as we finished the shopping.

"Bummer. I would love that." At my stunned expression, she laughed. "That's the one thing I think would be cool about being famous, just dressing up in disguise to go fill up the gas tank or grab midnight snacks."

"That's what you think would be cool about being famous? Not the adoration?"

"Ugh, no," she shuddered. "I'd be happy for people who know me to adore me, but strangers? No offense, that feels creepy."

"It is a bit. But I'm an athlete so I know why they love me. I win games and that gives them bragging rights over other hockey fans."

"Fair point. I guess that would be pretty cool to have people fist-bumping you at the grocery store. *Good game,*" she said in a gruff voice meant to be a hockey fan. "*Totally sick goal, Alex.*"

I stopped and just stared at this strange woman. She stopped and looked up at me, her blue eyes serious for a beat before she erupted in a fit of laughter that definitely drew a few stares. "You are a strange, strange woman Sasha."

"Thanks," she replied with a genuine smile, not at all offended by my assessment of her.

She was a strange woman, though. Instead of sitting inside the cool truck with Dixie, she kept an eye on her while she helped the workers load everything into the vehicle, ordering them around as if she was the boss. Every last one of them obeyed her commands with a smile.

"Thank you guys so much for the assist. I really appreciate it." She beamed that wide, full-lipped smile at them and I knew they would have followed her into battle. Hell, I might've gone with them.

On the trip home, all I could think about was that shopping for baby items was the most fun I'd ever had with a woman outside the bedroom. And wasn't that a sad state of affairs?

Maybe Jack was right and I needed to get my personal life in order, and not just because of the impact it could have on future endorsement deals. The problem was I met very few women like Sasha, and she was, well she was completely and totally off-limits.

Strictly off-limits.

Chapter 10

Sasha

"Come on, sweet girl, let's get you into the swing." I smiled like a proud mama when she kicked her legs excitedly and I set her in the swing. She started babbling when I adjusted the seat so she could see the world around her. "All good?"

Dixie's arms and legs kicked happily and when the swing began to move, she laughed. The sound was so sweet and joyful it warmed my heart.

"Good for you." I smiled at her and rubbed her soft, downy hair.

A loud knock sounded on the door startling me, but it was just one quick rap so I relaxed. Moments later, dozens of loud, successive knocks pounded against the door. Dixie whimpered at the loud, aggressive sound and I stared at the door for a long moment. I already knew there was a short list of people pre-approved to access the penthouse, but I also knew that Dixie's mother had managed to bypass that system. When Dixie's whimpers grew in intensity I knew soon she would be crying so I went to the door and tapped the camera on the wall, which revealed Jack's angry face.

I inhaled deeply and let it out slowly before I opened the door. "Jack."

"Where is he?" Jack's expression was furious as his head swung from left to right as if he thought Alex might be hiding from him.

"I don't know, Jack." I went to Dixie and picked her up to stop her from crying. "We just came out there. Is everything all right?"

"No!" He roared so loudly a vein sprang up on his forehead. "Everything is *not* all right! Where the hell is Alex? Alex," he called out before I could tell him that I had no idea where Alex might be.

"He's right here," Alex growled, rubbing his eyes, looking like he was ready for a photo shoot for expensive pajamas. His abs and his chest, bronzed with a light dusting of hair were distracting as hell, so I turned my attention to a still whimpering Dixie. "What's going on," he asked and took Dixie from me, laying her against his chest. She settled down instantly.

Lucky girl.

Jack sucked in a big breath of air and I took a step away from the two men, sensing an emotional volcano about to erupt. Jack let out the breath and produced a stack of newspapers and magazines, waving them around like a madman.

"I asked you to do one damn thing! One goddamned thing," he growled. "Keep her," he pointed at the baby in his arms, "under wraps. You have all this space, a nanny and a rooftop that's better than half the damn parks in the city and you couldn't do the one fucking thing I asked." He shook his head and finally dropped the papers on the table. "Not only do you not keep her under wraps, you three make an adorable fucking family!"

My eyes widen when I finally see what has Jack so riled up. It's a photo of me and Alex, laughing and smiling at each other with total adoration. He had one hand cradling Dixie's back as if he'd been doing it for months. It's totally out of context, but I was there, and I knew we were just laughing at some silly joke and I still thought we looked like a couple.

"What...who would do this?"

Jack laughed. "For crying out loud, woman, will you please do a simple internet search and learn who the hell he is!" His angry words startled me, but more than that I felt silly because he was right. I knew Alex was a professional athlete but I didn't want to taint what I knew about him by reading gossip. He turned back to Alex. "One thing," he repeated, holding up his index finger.

Alex's broad shoulders sank in resignation. "I know I screwed up, but it was a last minute problem and it couldn't be helped." He told him about the messed up order and the quick fix. "Babies need a lot of shit, and I couldn't let her go without another day. I'm her father."

He flashed another of his charming smiles and I couldn't help the smile that crossed my own face.

For a guy like Jack, I was sure Alex's attitude was infuriating.

"You can afford to hire someone to do this kind of shit for you, which I have been telling you for years. Your stubbornness has finally caught up to you, and now we need to deal with this."

"Deal with what?" I snorted the question and folded my arms. "From what you've said people take photos of Alex all that time. They'll think I'm an adoring fan and move on." Right?

"Wrong," he went to the coffee table, spreading out the magazines so they were all visible. "This isn't something a quick press release can fix. People are already asking questions about you and the baby," he pointed at me as if I was the cause of this. "They're speculating that you're his secret girlfriend and the baby is your love child. We have to fix it. Now."

"Jack," Alex began but his agent stopped him with a hand.

"Twenty million dollars, Alex."

Twenty million dollars? That was a lot of money and even though my curiosity burned, I told myself I didn't want to know what it was about. This was his business, not mine. I reached for Dixie and kissed the top of her head.

"Dixie and I will get out of your way and let you talk business. Good luck," I told Alex and walked away.

"Don't run too far, nanny. You're in this too."

I froze and turned slowly, shaking my head. "My job is to take care of Dixie, that's it. I signed your paper promising I wouldn't talk about any of this, and I won't. You're welcome."

Alex held up his hands, showing off sculpted biceps. "How are we going to fix this and what does Sasha have to do with it?"

Excellent question.

"I'll get back to you on that when I've worked out the details. Both of you." His gaze bounced back and forth between us before he let out an anguished moan and marched out of the penthouse like a man on death row.

"That went well," I said sarcastically, because what I really wanted to say to him was, *I told you so.*

He glared at me as if he could read my mind and pointed a finger in my direction. "Don't even think about saying it, Sasha."

I bit back a grin. "I'm not thinking about saying anything," I lied.

A low growl erupted and Alex opened his mouth to say something but snapped it shut. He shook his head and did it again, before he groaned in frustration.

"I'm going to work out." He stomped from the room, a cloud of expensive cologne and anxiety in his wake.

I held Dixie close and when I was sure I was alone, I laughed.

Chapter 11

Alex

Working out. Training.

That was the only thing I did for the past three days other than spend time with Dixie, because news of me and Sasha was everywhere. I'd made the mistake of leaving the penthouse—on my own—and the first newsstand I came to was covered in images of me and Sasha from that baby store. Online was, of course, worse by about ten country miles.

There were comparisons of Sasha and Tatiana everywhere, from their fashion choices to the way I interacted with them. The consensus so far was that I was in lust with Tatiana but Sasha was my soul mate. It was totally out of hand, and after that first day, leaving the penthouse without security wasn't possible so I spent my days working out, training and going over last season's games.

A prisoner in my own home.

Still, the season started soon and I couldn't afford to

start with an injury so I couldn't overdo it. I stepped back from the weight bag and wiped my forehead before leaving the gym to go in search of water.

"Hey."

Sasha looked up from where she was carefully feeding Dixie a tiny spoon of orange mush. "Hey. Good workout?" Her brows dipped in concern but she kept it to herself, which I appreciated.

"It was all right." I shrugged and guzzled a full bottle of water before tossing it into the recycling bin under the sink.

"Isn't there such a thing as overtraining?" I glared at her and she laughed. "Forget I asked."

Forget. As if I could. She was the reason being stuck at home was such a problem. She walked around in perfectly appropriate outfits for a nanny, but in my mind they were X-rated lacy and silky things that I unwrapped from her sinful curves. Every smile was an invitation, and that husky, lyrical laugh? It was too fucking much to handle without a release.

"I'm fine," I growled.

"Okay," she said in a high-pitched voice before she shrugged at my response and turned back to Dixie.

"What are you feeding her?"

"Broccoli and sweet potatoes," she answered without turning back to me, which I deserved.

"Is there any left?" I asked in a grouchy tone.

"There might be," Henrietta said as she entered the

kitchen with Jack on her heels. "If you ask nicely," she added with a teasing grin.

"Please?"

"Of course," she said as she brushed past me and made her way to the stove. "Jack is here," she added as an afterthought for the sole fact it would piss him off.

My gaze lifted from Henrietta to Jack who wore a satisfied smile. "What or who put that smile on your face?"

"I did, of course," he said as if that was obvious. "I'm a genius," he crowed, and even though in that moment I couldn't say why, unease settled in my gut.

"Not to toot your own horn or anything," Henrietta grumbled under her breath but she was loud enough to be heard.

Jack frowned.

Sasha snorted a laugh.

"Not even you can piss me off right now, Henri."

Henrietta bristled at the hated nickname and glared at Jack over her shoulder. "Watch it, boy."

Jack laughed again and turned to me, his eyes bright and excited. "I've got it all figured out, Alex. Every base covered."

I folded my arms, ready to listen, even though that pesky feeling in my gut hadn't gone anywhere. If anything, it only intensified.

"I'm listening." A low chime sounded in the distance but I maintained my focus on Jack and whatever plan he'd cooked up to get the world to stop asking about Sasha and Dixie.

"What in the hell is going on?" Sasha's voice sounded angry and confused and when I turned to see what had upset her, all I saw was fire burning in her blue eyes.

"That's what I wanted to talk to you about, both of you," Jack began.

Sasha stood, making sure Dixie was secure in her highchair before she marched across the kitchen and got in Jack's face. Her blue eyes were wide and furious as she poked her finger against his five hundred dollar shirt.

"Why does the internet think that the 'mysterious raven haired woman' is Alex Witter's baby mama and bride-to-be? Huh, Jack? Why?"

It took a second for her words to sink in, but when they did I turned to him. "Jack." It was the only thing I could manage at the moment.

"Yeah Jack," Sasha said over and over as she continued to poke him. "What did you do?"

Jack's eyes were wide and he looked at me for help, but I shook my head, effectively telling him he was on his own.

"Start. Talking. Now." I'd never heard Sasha sound so menacing or act so tough. It was seriously hot, which was the worst thing to be thinking in that moment.

"Okay," he growled and smacked Sasha's hand away from his chest. "Put that damn thing away, will ya?" He rubbed at his chest before putting a good distance between him and the pissed off nanny. "That's what I came here to talk to you about, both of you."

"You said that already."

Jack's eyes widened and he took another step back until the table and Dixie stood as barriers between him and Sasha. "I have a plan. It's quite genius actually, and neither of you can say no because the wheels are already in motion."

"Wheels?"

Jack nodded, getting excited again as he detailed his plan. "I may have admitted to a few gossip rags that you and Sasha are engaged but have been keeping it under wraps because she wants a private life."

"Why would you do that!" Sasha cried out. "It's an easy lie to uncover."

"Only if it's not a lie," he said with a smile. "You and Alex, from this moment forward are engaged. Betrothed. Promised to each other or however else you want to put it."

"We're not even dating," she tried because she didn't know Jack the way that I did. She didn't know yet that it was useless to argue with him.

"No one knows that for sure. Who's going to tell them, Henrietta?"

"This is ridiculous," she began as Dixie started to make her displeasure at being ignored known. She walked to the little girl to pick her up and I had to smile at Jack's frightened expression. "Just tell them I'm his nanny and be done with it."

"That's not possible," Jack shot back, his tone hard and firm. "The real story is unsavory, and after the whole Tatiana thing, this will all seem rather gross. No offense," he said and shot me a sympathetic smile.

"None taken."

"There's too much money at risk to play this any other way. Believe me I spent most of the past two days playing out different scenarios. This one is the best."

If that's what Jack believed, it was probably true. He was a shrewd businessman and not at all sentimental, which meant this was the way.

"Okay. How will it work?"

Sasha glared at me as if I'd betrayed her while she bounced Dixie in her arms. "You must be sharing a pipe if you think this is going to work. What about Dixie's mom, the woman who slept with Alex and gave birth to this little girl? She could come out and deny the whole thing with receipts, and I'm guessing that would be worse than the truth." She closed her eyes and inhaled Dixie's baby scent as if it was a kind of calming elixir. "And what if it turns out that Dixie isn't even his child?"

Jack stared at Sasha with a smile. "She's good. If you get tired of the nanny gig, come talk to me."

Her gaze narrowed in Jack's direction but I'd tuned them out, because my mind and my heart were focused on the thought that Dixie might not be mine. It had only been a few days, just over a week since she entered my life, but now I couldn't imagine her anywhere else.

"That's not an answer," she said in a voice so calm that it sent ice barreling through my veins.

"That's why I didn't come by yesterday to warn you before your name and face were splashed all over the internet, I was waiting for this." He pulled an envelope from the inside of his jacket and handed it to me. "It came in yesterday afternoon."

I stared at the envelope that held my entire future in it. *It's just some results. Yes or no, maybe a few percentages. Nothing more than that,* I told myself.

This is what I wanted, what I needed to know to figure out what my next step would be. Not too long ago I told Sasha I didn't know what outcome I wanted, but as I stared at the envelope sandwiched between Jack's fingers, I knew that was a lie. I wanted Dixie to be mine. I wanted to be her father and her protector. I needed her as much as she needed me.

"Alex." Sasha's soft voice tugged me from my frozen position in the middle of the kitchen. She placed a hand on my arm until our gazes collided, hers was filled with concern and worry.

"Take the results," she said and plucked the envelope from Jack's hand and put it in mine. "Go open this in private. Read it and then re-read it. Process your feelings before you do anything else."

I nodded at her suggestion and wrapped my fingers tightly around the envelope. "Yeah. I think I will."

"Go," she said softly and gave me a gentle shove.

I walked out of the kitchen and towards my bedroom, but not before I caught Jack's last words. "See? You two are already a good couple."

I shook my head. Jack wasn't wrong, so far Sasha and I were a good team. A team though, not a couple.

In the quiet of my room I peeled the flap off the envelope and slid the paper out until it fluttered to the floor. I picked it up with shaky hands and read over the results at least a half dozen times until the truth settled in my bones and down to my soul.

Dixie was my daughter. She was mine.

Whatever else was true, that was settled. I could move forward with that knowledge and plan accordingly. I sat there and did as Sasha had instructed, I thought about the results and how I felt about them. I thought about the pros and cons of Jack's plan, devoting a solid ten minutes before I got to my feet and rejoined Jack and Sasha.

We had a future to plan.

Chapter 12

Sasha

"This is good for everyone." Jack flashed what was supposed to be a charming smile, but it was borderline smarmy. "Seriously, we'll negotiate a big fat sum for pretending while you continue to do your job and take care of this little one."

I understood what Jack was saying, and I really didn't want Alex to get in trouble when he was only trying to make sure his little girl had everything she needed. But the downside was a dealbreaker.

"I don't lie."

"Ever?" His question was so incredulous and the smirk on his face made me want to smack him. "You never lie?"

"No. The truth is easier to remember and no one gets hurt." Mostly. The truth could hurt a lot, but it hurt worse after a lifetime of lies. "Sorry. I'm not agreeing to deceive the world."

He leaned forward with that car salesman look on his

face. "I mean you're not exactly the paragon of truth, are you? Playing at being a nanny despite who your family is."

"I'm not playing at anything. I've been doing this job for years, I earned it and I'm damn good at it." I wished that looks could kill, because I really wanted to hurt him for that comment.

"No offense," he said and held up his hands defensively. "And you don't have to worry about lying anyway because this marriage will be one hundred percent real."

"Real." The word fell from my lips as if it was foreign, as if it held no meaning. "You mean that your plan is for us to get married for real? In front of a preacher and everything?" I shook my head because this was now getting even more ridiculous.

He shrugged. "You can choose about who officiates the thing with Alex, as long as it's real and legal, I don't care."

"This is crazy."

"It's not, actually." Alex's deep voice sounded behind me and I turned to see he was still not wearing a shirt, but there was a difference in him. He seemed settled or content, something like that, but I didn't know him well enough to know which. "A fake engagement or marriage would be worse for me if anyone found out."

Dammit, and there goes the guilt creeping in, as if I had anything to feel guilty about. This was Alex's and Jack's fault, but I was the one feeling guilty for not jumping into this crazy plan with both feet.

"Listen Sasha, people do this all the time," Jack explained. "They marry for a variety of reasons and they have for centuries. Love is just one reason, but you know better than most that it's not always at the top of the list when planning a marriage."

I clenched my jaws so hard I heard them grinding inside my head as I shot hate darts at him.

"Don't get upset. Of course, I looked into you and your past. That's another reason you're perfect."

"Yeah? Enlighten me." Whatever he thought he knew was only what the family publicist wanted the world to know.

"Your parents got married because it was the joining of two powerful families. Maybe over time they grew to love each other, but it wasn't a love match."

"What?" Alex dropped down beside me and took Dixie from my arms, leaning back on the sofa to give her a comfortable and warm surface to snooze.

"You didn't know that your nanny is from a rich family?" Jack laughed. "She has plenty of money of her own, which means no one will dare accuse her of being a gold digger."

Alex's frown darkened. "You said your parents were rich, not you."

"I'm not," I insisted.

"But you have a trust fund."

"You do?" Alex sat up, but when Dixie squirmed he leaned back and gave her a soothing pat on the back.

"I have one, yes. But I haven't touched it in years. I live on my salary."

Jack clapped his hands together loudly and the sound

startled Dixie from her sleep. "That's what makes you so perfect. A rich girl working as a nanny and living off her meager salary. The people will love you."

"The salary is hardly meager," I grumbled, so annoyed I wanted to throw something at Jack's smiling face.

"You're rich," Alex said again.

"Focus," Jack snapped. "You're perfect for this Sasha, whether you like it or not. What's it going to take to get you to say yes?"

I didn't have a price. There was nothing I wanted, except this. I didn't want to be real fake married to Alex. I turned to Alex with a plea in my gaze for him to be the reasonable one right now.

"Why can we just tell them that I'm the nanny because you're a busy professional and Dixie's mother is no longer with us, or whatever. The point is just tell them I'm the nanny."

Alex shook his head even before I finished speaking. "Sasha, look at me."

I didn't want to look at him. The sight of him shirtless and holding Dixie was too much. It was what my friend Toni would call an ovary-exploder. "Alex."

"Jack's right, it has to be this way."

"Why? There are literally like, ten other options."

"Because no one will believe that you're just the nanny."

"But that's the truth!" My voice grew in pitch until I was sure there were dogs in the city going crazy right now.

This was all so strange, and I was slowly starting to feel like I was in an alternate universe.

"You're right. It's the truth, and it would be believable, if it was anyone other than me." He looked away. "Anyone who knows my reputation won't believe that I could share a home with a beautiful woman and keep it platonic. They'll just keep speculating and they'll believe we're together even if we tell them otherwise. Let's give them the story they're desperate to believe."

Dammit that did make a weird sort of sense. "And you're all right with this, just marrying a virtual stranger?"

He nodded, but I didn't believe him.

"Liar. You're all right with not dating or sleeping with anyone else for the duration of our marriage?"

His mouth did the guppie dance of uncertainty and I knew the truth. "I can do it." His gaze met mine and I saw the truth in those depths. For his career, Alex would do anything, and that was something I respected the hell out of him for.

"I need to think about it." I wanted to help Alex, and Dixie, but I didn't want to get roped into a situation that was destined to end badly.

"You can't tell anyone," Jack growled, an unwelcome reminder of his presence.

"Too bad. I have to tell Serenity. She's my boss and this little charade will only last a few months, but after that I still have a career to think about. Just because you don't respect it, doesn't make it invalid."

"I was raised by nannies and have great respect for

them." His words were fierce and revealed a new layer to the annoying agent. "Second, this isn't just a few months, Sasha. We're talking one to two years. At least."

"At least?"

He nodded. "Yes. I'm not ruining Alex's brand on some shotgun wedding and divorce. Like I said, you will be well compensated, however you choose. Think about it."

Alex stood and blocked my path. "Please Sasha, just think about it. Seriously think about it." He pulled out a sheet of paper. "She's mine. Dixie is my daughter and I think this plan is the best way forward."

I nodded.

"I don't want her to grow up and see the shitty things people write about her or her mother's relationship with me."

Double dammit. "Yeah, okay. I said I'll think about it." I reached for Dixie and Alex stepped back.

"Think long and hard," he instructed. "No distractions. Just think of being married to all this for the next couple of years."

I laughed. "I might be getting the better end of the stick," I joked. "If I agree so don't get too excited."

His smile fell and his gaze darkened. "Agree to disagree."

Uh oh.

Warning bells went off and I stepped back. "I'll have an answer for you tomorrow."

Chapter 13

Alex

I woke up earlier than usual the next day, anticipation of Sasha's answer sat like a weight on my chest.

Had I done enough to convince her to get on board with Jack's crazy plan? Should I have done more, fattened the pot like Jack had recommended, or applied a little pressure with my charm? I didn't know, but I wanted her to come to the decision on her own, not necessarily under coercion.

I stared at the ceiling for about fifteen minutes before I sat up, smacked the switch to open the blinds and bathed the room in sunlight. It was still early, and though I wanted to hit the gym, I stepped out of my room and stared at the other end of the hall. On the other side of that door was the woman who held my future and my continued wealth in her hands. I smiled and headed in that direction, not to pressure Sasha, at least not overtly.

Instead of knocking, I turned at the last minute to Dixie's room, figuring that I could help Sasha while spending some time with my daughter.

My daughter. I didn't doubt it, but now that I knew it for certain, it all felt right. She was mine. I frowned at the empty crib. She was also gone.

I figured she was in the kitchen having breakfast so that's where I headed next. "Morning, Henrietta."

She looked over her shoulder at me with one eyebrow arched and a grin on her face. "Dixie's in the room with Sasha. Been in there all morning."

All morning? "It's barely past eight," I insisted at the implication that I was late to rise.

"Dixie woke up early with a tummy ache so Sasha got up with her, soothed her and brought her to her room. Been there a long time," she said slowly. "You know anything about that?"

I shrugged because telling Henrietta the truth was something I'd gone back and forth on since last night. There was no way to keep her in the dark, but I didn't want to tell her anything until I had Sasha's answer. "I do."

"Well, you want to tell me or should I guess?" She nodded for me to take a seat and turned back to the stove.

I sat and let my mind wander. Of course Sasha wanted time to herself and that was why she was holed up in her room. It was a big thing she's been asked to do, which put her in the position of getting anything she wanted, and that was scary as fuck to think about. Yeah, I needed a sounding board.

"The tabloids are all over me and Sasha being a couple, and Dixie is our love child."

"Oh, I know all about it. You look good together, like a real couple."

"Yeah I noticed," I grumbled and told her all about Jack's plan for us to get married for real and stay married. "Is it ridiculous?"

Henrietta turned from the stove with a plate piled high with food, and since training started soon, it was all healthier alternatives. "That depends. Are you planning to be married in name only, or will it be real in the bedroom too?"

I laughed and shook my head. "No," I admitted even though I would love nothing more than to take Sasha to bed.

"Why not?" She set the plate down in front of me with a knowing smile. "You might as well go for it since you can't keep your eyes off her, and since you're determined to wander the house shirtless, she can't keep her eyes off you either." She laughed and shook her head.

"What can I say, Henrietta? I like beautiful things." And Sasha was a very beautiful woman, but also off-limits. "She hasn't given me an answer yet." I tapped my fingers anxiously on the counter before I picked up the fork and took a big bite of scrambled egg whites.

"She'll say yes because she's a sweetheart, but maybe you ought to do something to sweeten the deal."

I frowned. "She has a blank check, Henrietta."

"Don't be dense, Alex. I'm talking about a ring. A big

fat one that will make her eyes sparkle with joy, that will make her feel special even though this is all transactional."

Transactional.

I hated that word, but I couldn't deny the truth of it because I was giving her something to compensate her for giving me her life for a year. Possibly two.

"You're right, Henrietta."

"I usually am," she said smugly and set a platter of extra food on the counter in front of me. "Good luck."

"Thanks," I grunted, eating while I thought about whether or not I wanted to buy my real fake wife a ring. A ring. Would she read too much into it, or would she appreciate it like Henrietta said?

By the time I made it halfway through a second helping, I had my answer. I called the best jeweler in the city.

"Neal, I need a ring. Something nice and big, for a woman not like your usual customer. Think you can help?"

He laughed. "Never thought I'd see the day, but yes, Mr. Witter, I can help." Neal was my go to guy for goodbye trinkets when a woman tried to make things more than they were. Broaches, earrings, necklaces and bracelets were my thing. Not rings.

Never rings.

"Excellent. Meet me in an hour." Apparently I was about to buy an engagement ring.

Chapter 14

Sasha

Why is this so hard?

I mean, I spent all night lying in this comfortable bed staring at the ceiling making a mental pros and cons list for marrying Alex Witter.

The pros were that this would be something I could do to help someone and it would give Dixie's young life some stability. Then again, on the other side of that coin was that this relationship had a guaranteed expiration date which wasn't all that great for stability. Which brought me to the next con, which was my inconvenient attraction to my maybe future husband. I could deal with that, I was sure I could, but the problem was that Alex was more than a gorgeous face and a hot body, he was a hard worker, a nice guy who was shaping up to be a good dad.

That could lead to me getting attached, which was a short path to getting my heart broken.

I could do this, I tried to convince myself as Dixie slumbered in my arms. I could just bury that attraction down so deep that it would never be unearthed.

"I guess I have my answer."

With that decided, I kissed the top of Dixie's head and settled her in the crib with the monitor watching over her. I hooked the other end in my back pocket and went in search of my husband-to-be.

It shouldn't be too hard since Alex hadn't left the house in more than a week. Apparently the press had been camped out in front of the building, eager to get photos of the city's newest celebrity couple.

It was laughable really, because I was no one's idea of a celebrity, but apparently being close to one made you a celebrity by default. But thanks to the tabloids I knew that Alex was around here somewhere. He wasn't in his office, gym or in his bedroom which left the kitchen.

"Looking for Alex?" Henrietta smiled as if she knew something, which was unsettling.

"Yes. Have you seen him?"

"He's up on the roof. I'll keep an eye on Dixie."

"Thanks." I held up the monitor. "I have this too just in case you have other things to do."

She smiled and patted my shoulder. "You're a sweetheart, Sasha. We could use more of that around here." Without another word, she shuffled off probably to hold Dixie close and get some of her sweet baby magic.

I smiled at just how eager she was to spend more time

with the little girl. That was a good thing, having more people to love that baby. I vowed to make an effort to give her more time with Dixie, even if that meant pitching in around the penthouse.

But first, business.

I made my way up to the roof using the staircase in an effort to burn off the last of my nerves before I approached Alex. At the door, I nearly ran into a middle-aged man with a gorgeous head of silver hair.

"Excuse me."

He smiled wide and stepped to the side. "No, excuse me, ma'am." He nodded and stepped through the door.

The sound of his humming faded slowly as I turned to scan the rooftop until my gaze landed on Alex. He sat with his legs extended and his face turned towards the sky. Damn he really was a handsome man. Unfairly good looking, especially when combined with his charm and his body.

He's okay, I tried to convince myself. That was bull. He was stunning, physically perfect and this was a truly terrible idea.

But you've already made up your mind.

It was a poor justification at best. The decision hadn't been voiced yet, which meant there was no agreement, nothing to back out of as of this moment. Yet my feet moved across the fake grass, not stopping until just a few feet separated me and Alex.

"Hey."

Alex moved slowly, not at all concerned, which for some reason, made this a little easier. He sat up and let his gaze wander over my body until our gazes met, and he smiled wide.

"Sasha. What's up?"

What's up?

I couldn't help it, I laughed. I laughed long and hard until all the tension seeped out and I felt solid and settled in my choice. "Don't pretend like you're not impatient to hear my answer when we both know that you are."

He slumped forward, still smiling and released a weighty sigh. "Good thing you're getting to know me so well already. Okay," he said more to himself than to me. "I'm listening. What's your answer?" His jaw clenched and his nostrils flared, anxiety was written all over his body because my answer mattered to him.

There was no point drawing it out. I wasn't a dramatic sort of person and this wasn't real. It was legal but not emotional.

"I'm going to do it."

Alex whooped as he got to his feet and pulled my chest flush against his, lifting me off my feet as he swung me in about a dozen circles.

"Thank you, Sasha!"

I tried like hell to ignore the way it felt to have all of those considerably hard muscles pressed against my decidedly softer body. He felt good and smelled even better, masculine and clean, like the forest and leather. His grip on me was tight. It was strong and it was comforting. I felt safe, which wasn't how I should have felt around a man as dangerous—to my heart—as Alex Witter.

"I have conditions," I blurted out, which effectively stopped the spinning and his revelry as I intended it to.

Alex sobered and set me on my feet before taking a few steps back. "Of course you have conditions. What are they?" He was so serious it was almost comical.

I smiled because I was sure he and Jack had prepared for me to ask for millions of dollars, a house and a few luxury vehicles. It's what Tatiana would have asked for, probably the other women he'd been linked to over the years too. I'd finally looked them up last night. I needed to know what I would be getting myself into, if I decided to marry him.

"You look worried."

He shrugged. "You have the power here, Sasha."

"Heady words for a simple nanny to hear," I joked before deciding to put him out of his misery. "The first thing I want is one hundred thousand dollars donated to the Children of Alcoholics for every year that we're married."

Surprise flashed in his eyes along with about twenty different questions that he kept to himself as he nodded.

"Second, I want you to start a charity in your name for underprivileged kids who show athletic promise but lack the resources to participate. I think half a million dollars is a good starting point, but you can choose how to continue it going forward."

Alex nodded, thumbs hooked through his beltloops. "Okay. That's an odd ask, but sure, done. What else?"

What else? "Isn't that enough? I've asked you to spend nearly one million dollars of your hard earned money, Alex."

He laughed and shook his head. "I expected to pay at least that much for each year of our marriage. Jack was willing to go up to three mil."

My eyes bugged out at the insane numbers. Sure, I grew up surrounded by money, but I was too young to appreciate this level of spending. "Well that's all I want. Agree to those terms and I'm your intended. Do you agree?" He'd already agreed, but I needed to hear him say it out loud.

"I agree," he said, nodding and smiling because he'd definitely gotten a good deal. "I doubt I'll have a problem getting Jack to agree to those terms."

"Perfect." I thought I might feel different now that it was official. I was an engaged woman, but I didn't feel any different. *Of course you don't, this isn't a love match.* "Now that we have that settled, I think we ought to set some ground rules." It was the other thing that kept me up all night possibly even more than whether or not to marry Alex.

He frowned. "Didn't we just do that?" Realization dawned, and it was fascinating to watch Alex transform. His laidback persona vanished and his jaws took on a hard set, his brow furrowed and his beautiful mouth pinched into a frown.

I shook my head at his question. "Not exactly. We settled the terms but now we need to decide about more personal matters such as sex. Dating. Public displays of affection." The look on his face was absolutely priceless.

I felt a small measure of pride that I'd managed to shock this man into silence.

Chapter 15

Alex

I shook my head because it felt as if my brain had malfunctioned. I could have sworn Sasha said she wanted to talk about sex. Sex and dating and getting physical in public.

"Alex, are you okay?"

I looked at the concern in her eyes and smiled. This was Sasha. We didn't know each other very well—yet—but her conditions gave me hope about trusting her.

"Sorry, I stopped listening after you said sex." I flashed a teasing grin because I didn't want her to be uncomfortable.

With a roll of her eyes, she reluctantly returned my smile. "Focus, Alex."

I wanted to focus, I truly did, but now that the word had fallen from those luscious pink lips, it was hard not to think of the implications. I'd been trying not to think about Sasha and sex in the same sentence, but now it was all I could think about. Having her under me, on top of me. From behind, gripping her curves as I made her scream my name.

"Alex," she growled, snapping her fingers in front of my face. "Focus."

"Focus." Focus on sex with Sasha. I could do that. "Between practice and games, plus your responsibilities to Dixie, I figure three times a week should satisfy us both." More if I could convince her.

She sputtered and shook her head, seemingly perplexed when she was the one who brought it up.

"I meant sex with other people."

"Other people?" I frowned. "You're my fiancée, and soon to be my wife, I can't fuck around on you. I won't." As a single man who hadn't made any promises to anyone, I never felt bad about taking a beautiful woman to bed, making sure we both had fun before we went our separate ways. But this was different, this was the next level. Sasha was an entirely different entity.

Sasha's blue eyes widened in surprise at my vehemence, but then she laughed. "I get what you're saying Alex, but you're not choosing to marry me. We're not dating and we haven't even kissed to start laying out details of our sex life. For all you know, we're totally incompatible in the bedroom."

The moment she mentioned kissing, my eyes went to her mouth. It was lush, that was for damn sure. She had plump lips the color of watermelon, pink with a hint of shine. Her bottom lip was plumper, and her top lip had a deep bow that gave her face more character.

"Alex," she said. My name came out low and breathy, and I understood what she was feeling because I felt it too.

Attraction.

Arousal.

I closed the gap between us and pulled her close, revelling in the feel of all those curves mashed up against me. Her tits were soft and plump, a bit more than a handful. Her hard nipples dug into my ribs and when her breath hitched, we were even closer.

"We can remedy part of that right now," I told her with a low voice, barely able to conceal my own arousal.

"W-what?"

"The kiss. You're right, we haven't even kissed yet, and here we are about to be married. Best to be sure, don't you think?"

Sasha shook her head no, but her tongue slipped out and slicked across her lips as if in preparation for what was to come. "We don't need to."

"Oh, but we do."

"We do?" Her eyes were glazed over with a lust she tried hard to fight. "I mean, no we don't."

I smiled. "Then step back and we won't."

The pulse in her throat fluttered quickly to go along with her shallow breaths. She wanted to back away, to avoid the kiss, but she knew as I did, it was inevitable.

I lowered my head. "Last chance, Sasha."

Her body relaxed against mine and her hands settled

on my shoulders. It was as much of a green light as I would get and I lowered my head until our mouths touched.

I'd meant it to be a short kiss, one to show her the chemistry that was always there between us, just waiting to be explored. But one touch of our lips and the spark was lit. She tasted of strawberries and mint and when she opened her mouth to me and our tongues touched it was explosive.

One hand speared through her thick black waves, tilting her head back so I could devour her completely while the other hand slid down to cup her hip and pull her closer. She was so fucking soft everywhere, her hip in my hand, her tits and her belly pressed against my body so I felt every hitch of her breath, every shuddery breath.

Her tongue danced with mine, tentative at first and then with more intensity. She pushed her body against mine and looped her arms around my neck, pulling me down, silently begging for more.

Sasha moaned and my control snapped. One hand slipped past her hip and gripped one ample ass cheek because I had to know if it was as soft and feminine as it looked. Just like I knew her tits would be, it was more than a handful and I wanted more.

I wanted all of her.

Dammit, I just wanted to show her that we would be compatible in the bedroom, but I miscalculated how much I would want her after one taste. Now I had to have her, and that could be a special form of hell if she wasn't on board.

But then her hands fisted in my hair and pulled me closer, and suddenly I didn't give a damn about anything but the next swipe of her tongue while my hands roamed all over her flesh. My hand slipped under the hem of her shirt, my thumb swiped across the silky flesh of her lower back and my fingers did the same at her soft belly. Shit, she was so soft, so utterly feminine, and it was almost too late to turn back.

Almost simultaneously, we pulled back and stared at each other. I smiled down at Sasha while she looked up at me with a stunned expression that I felt down to my toes. The kiss had stunned me too, but someone had to be clear headed right now, and despite her kiss-swollen lips and glazed over expression, it had to be me.

"Now, we've kissed. It was hot as fuck. Right?"

Sasha nodded and one hand left my hair and went to her mouth as if she wanted to imprint my kiss, my taste right there forever. "Yeah," she sighed and nodded, eyes still filled with shock. "Hot." She took a few steps back and shook her head, a new resolve settled around her. "Public affection is fine, touching and kissing and all that, but no sex. We can't have sex, not with each other. Just be discreet." She ran off, thinking that was the end of the conversation.

But she forgot she was dealing with a professional athlete and I caught up with her easily. "Sasha, wait."

"I can't, Alex." She was scared.

"Why not?" A thought occurred to me. "Are you a virgin?"

She laughed. "Hardly, but I'm not as experienced as you are. It's just, I can't do casual sex. I'm not judging you, hell right now I really wish I could do it."

That made me feel better. A little. "Boyfriend or girlfriend?"

"No," she sighed. "You're a nice guy Alex. Hot *and* nice, which is a bad combination."

I shook my head. "Now I'm confused. Explain."

She smiled. "If you were a jerk, maybe this could work, sex between us. But so far you've been nice and sweet, and you're trying to do right by Dixie."

My frown grew. "Those all sound like compliments."

"They are, and that's the problem. Physically you're already irresistible which would be fine if you were a jerk, but combined with your other aforementioned attributes, it's a big problem for me."

"I'm still not getting it, Sasha."

"Exactly," she motioned at me. "You're used to women who see what you have and want it so they do whatever it takes to get you. I already know that you don't do serious or commitments, and I'm under no illusions that I'll be the woman to change that, which means I can't fall for you."

I took a step back. "What?"

She sighed and her face turned a bright shade of red. "That kiss was incredible and if we do more than that behind closed doors, this will feel like a real relationship, except it isn't. You didn't ask me to marry you because you love me and want to spend your life with me."

"We just met."

"I know," she laughed. "We'll be married for at least a year. Living together all that time and pretending we're in love for the world. Now if we take that to the bedroom it will feel real to me, but it won't be real, and when this is all over, I'll be crushed. I don't want to do that to myself and I don't want you to feel guilty about something that's not your fault. Understand?"

I nodded, but I didn't understand at all.

"Good," she said and rushed off the roof, leaving me hot and bothered, and confused as hell.

Chapter 16

Sasha

"You want to do *what?*"

My eyes bugged out of my head and I shook my head as if maybe I was still asleep and dreaming when Alex dropped down on the sofa beside me, legs propped up on the coffee table and his gaze softening towards Dixie before he turned to me.

"You heard me." He flashed a smile that was too charming by half, but the impact was the same as if he was mine. "I want us to date. We should date. We're already engaged, and we can date and get to know each other while we plan our wedding."

My gaze narrowed in his direction. I wanted to be flattered by his attention, his desire to date me, but I wasn't naïve.

"You want to date me so that we can have sex."

His head fell against my shoulder and he barked out a

loud, fully amused—maybe *too* amused—laugh. "At the risk of sounding like an arrogant jerk, I could probably seduce you without the dates. I've been told that I have certain charms. But I want to do it the right way. We can go on dates, and if you want to kiss me or more when the cameras aren't around, great. If you get to know me and you still don't want to touch me when the cameras aren't around, that's okay too."

"Ugh," I groaned and shoved him away from me. "Why do you have to be so reasonable?"

He laughed and bumped my shoulder. "I'm a reasonable guy, or I can be when it's the right thing."

I rolled my eyes. This was a bad idea. Everything about dating my fiancé sounded like a bad idea, not the least of which was because he was good-looking and charming and sweet. Did I mention the abs? They were a thing of beauty, and I'd be lying if I said I hadn't thought about licking each and every one of them. But that couldn't happen.

"Wouldn't it be easier to find a woman who could take the orgasms and walk away without feelings?"

"I'm not opposed to commitment," he said with a pout.

I laughed, because everything about his dating history indicated a man who was, at least, gun shy about committing to a woman.

"I'm not," he insisted. "The truth?"

I nodded. "Always."

He nodded, his gaze fixed on mine as he spoke. "I'm

not adverse to commitment, but the women who come into my orbit, they're vultures. I know what they want, and it isn't me beyond my body, face and my status. But that's okay, because I get what I want too. Just because I haven't found the right woman yet doesn't mean I'll be scared when I find her."

I understood that, and to a certain extent, I believed him. "I doubt I'm that woman, Alex." Despite my so-called pedigree, I wasn't wildly beautiful or successful, I wasn't a diplomat or a princess, or even all that accomplished. I was a simple woman happy with a simple life and Alex was anything but simple.

"Clearly I don't know who that woman is, but I think that I'll know her when I see her."

I roared with laughter, smacking a hand over my face to avoid waking Dixie. "So what you're saying is that your perfect woman is like porn, you can't define her, but you'll know her when you see her?"

"All that matters is that when I see her, I will stop at nothing to make her mine."

"Lucky girl," I murmured, certain that woman wasn't me.

His eyes sparkled and he leaned in. "So, Sasha, what do you say? Want to date me before we get married?"

Did I want to date him? Of course, I did. He was handsome and charming, sexy and sweet. But I couldn't. He wasn't for me. "I do, but I also think it's a terrible idea bound to end very badly for one of us."

"I don't know, Sasha. That sweet face combined with these killer curves has heartbreaker written all over it. For all your worrying, you might end up breaking my heart."

I laughed. "Anything is possible, but not always probable." Even the idea that he would fall for me and I would break his heart was just laughable, but I shrugged off that *not good enough* feeling and kept a smile on my face. "But since we have to do this anyway, you have a deal. Let's give it a shot." I held my hand out and waited for him to accept it.

Of course, Alex can't do anything the easy way and he takes my hand, pulling me so close I'm practically draped across his big body. "Deal," he whispered, his face so close that I felt his warm breath on my face.

The proximity pulled a shudder from me and my breath hitched. "You should probably let Jack know so he can do whatever it is he does about these things."

Alex's shoulders drooped and he let out a disappointed sigh though his smile never wavered. "Fine," he growled. "I can take a hint."

I laughed. "Yeah? Because somehow I don't think that's true."

With a defiant expression, Alex put some distance between us and stood, walking towards the front door. He turned with a slow smile before he disappeared down the hall.

My shoulders relaxed when Alex was out of sight. His presence always left me unsettled and wanting more than

I should. Whatever was going on between us, it was a temporary glitch. Distance would allow us both to get our heads on straight and realize that chemistry didn't mean much when it came to the long-term.

I heard heavy footsteps, and before I knew what was happening, Alex was there, standing in front of me with an intense look on his face that stole my breath. "Sasha," he growled, taking my hand to pull me to my feet, yanking me close so we were chest to chest. "Sorry, not sorry," he whispered and then his mouth was on mine.

Again.

I didn't want to want his kiss, but it was too intoxicating. The way his lips, strong and firm, moved against mine made me feel drunk. The feel of his hands on my hips and then my ass, was enticing. I felt beautiful and desired when I pushed against his chest and molded our bodies together.

He growled and gripped my hips, pulling me so close that not even air could pass between us. His tongue tangled with mine, led the dance as we consumed one another. I couldn't get enough of him or his taste, never mind the feel of his hard body pressed up against mine. It was heavenly, it was the hottest kiss of my life and I never wanted it to end, even though it shouldn't even have gotten started.

And then Alex slowed the kiss, it was no longer frenzied, but it was slow and deliberate. Every pass of his tongue was intentional with the sole purpose of driving me crazy, of wanting him more, which I didn't think was possible. But after the third or maybe the tenth pass of his tongue, I trembled with need as my fingers speared through his hair and pulled him closer.

Alex groaned, gripping my ass cheeks in his hands as he dipped me over his arm and continued to devour my mouth until I was nothing more than a puddle of desire. I couldn't say who pulled back first, me or Alex, but suddenly we were staring at each other with wide eyes and heaving chests.

"Sasha," he groaned.

I nodded because I knew what he was thinking and I felt the same way, but voicing it felt dangerous.

"Alex," I moaned as he pulled me closer for another kiss, just as hot but much shorter.

He pulled back with our hands clasped as he tilted my head back. "Sasha Turner, will you marry me?"

It wasn't over the top romantic, and I didn't need it to be, but somehow his simple request with his mussed hair and furrowed brow was enough.

"Um, Alex," I whispered as I looked down at the ring with the halo setting and a pink diamond set in the middle with tons of white diamonds surrounding it. "This is gorgeous. It's perfect." It wasn't too over the top, but it was stunning. "I love it."

"So is that a yes?" His lips tugged into a grin.

"Yes, Alex. I will marry you."

He slipped the ring on my finger and pressed a kiss to

the middle of my hand, emerald eyes sparkling with excitement. "See you later."

"I'll be right here," I said, trying to keep my voice light despite my racing heart and damp panties.

"Then I'll know right where to find you," he shot back with a wink and then disappeared out of the penthouse.

Right along with my peace.

Chapter 17

Alex

Jack stared at me as I finished laying out the details of my marriage arrangement with Sasha, mouth and eyes wide with shock as he shook his head in disbelief.

"Is she stupid?"

It was a fair question, and about exactly the response I expected from him. "No, she's not stupid."

"Are you sure?"

I nodded. "She wanted something good to come out of this, and if it makes you feel better, it's still a good chunk of change I have to part with." It wasn't a small amount by any stretch of the imagination, but it was far less than either of us had expected.

Jack shook his head but slowly a smile crept across his face. "I mean she could have gotten just about anything she wanted for this deal, and she chose two things that don't even benefit her. How odd." He shrugged it off, not at all fascinated by anyone who wasn't motivated by money or power. "I'll get the contracts drawn up before she changes her mind then."

I understood the way Jack thought, it was what made him good at what he did, but I didn't worry about Sasha changing her mind, not after that kiss. She might want to keep things platonic behind closed doors, but us coming together? It was inevitable. Surely she could see that, could feel it in the way our bodies arched into each other, stuck together like magnets. Couldn't she? If not, she would.

And soon.

"Now we need to start planning the wedding," Jack said, his voice snapping me out of my obsessive thoughts about Sasha. "The timeline should be a six month engagement while you plan the wedding, and two years of marriage before your hectic schedule becomes too much for Sasha and she leaves you and the baby."

I frowned. "I can't do that to her."

"She had her chance, Alex. Don't go soft on me now."

"It's not soft, Jack. It's called being a decent human being. You know the hate she'll get if she walks away from Dixie. It will devastate her." Shit, not to mention how Dixie will feel. Sasha will be the only mother she's ever known. "I need to think about that." It was just another reason to have alone time with Sasha.

"Fine, you figure out the details, all I ask is that you run it by me first. My only concern is your career, Alex." His dark gaze was serious and I knew he meant business.

"I know, but I've got the bandwidth to think about other things too."

He gave a sharp nod. "Fine, moving on. Kayla Crumbley."

My brows dipped in confusion. "Who?" I sat up straight, wondering what the hell my agent was up to now.

Jack flashed his car salesman smile and laughed. "She's the hottest new wedding planner to the stars."

"No." I shook my head.

"You have someone else in mind?" Jack laughed at the annoyed look I gave him. "Didn't think so. What's wrong with Kayla, oh wait, don't tell me she's one of your conquests."

"No, I don't know her at all." But an idea had started to spin in my head, and given Jack's whirlwind timeline, I knew I had to be smart. Sasha was reluctant to get close to me, and given my obsessive need to have her, I was starting to understand her perspective. "But I was just thinking…"

"Never a good thing," he mumbled under his breath, flashing a smile when I glared at him. "Out with it, Alex. Tell me of your grand plan," he said mockingly.

"Sasha and I should plan the wedding. Together." The more I played with it in my mind, the more certain I was that this was the way to go.

"What?" Jack shook his head. "You do remember that training starts in three days, right? You know, your actual job?" He shook his head some more and angrily tossed a pen on the desk between us. "What's really going on?"

Everything. "Nothing," I lied smoothly. "Okay, not

nothing. You do know that I'm more than a pretty face, don't you?"

He barked out a laugh as he relaxed against the expensive office chair. "Let's hear the plan before we start talking like that."

I smirked at him. "Okay, listen. Sasha and I will plan the wedding together and we'll do it publicly."

"Why in the hell would you do that? Oh hell, you like her don't you?"

"Of course, I like her. She is a perfectly likeable woman," I smiled sweetly. "But that's not what this is about." It was absolutely what it was about, but there was another part of the story. "If the world can see some of our love story play out, they won't ask so many questions, like where have I been hiding her and how did we meet? We'll give them enough good content that no one will dig into our relationship."

Jack's eyes sparkled. "I'm listening."

I smiled as my confidence grew, spitting out the details as they came to me. "The press will get some good photos of the happy couple, satisfying their bloodlust for more. But there's something else," I added because I knew this was the part that would appeal to Jack the most.

He rolled his eyes. "Cut the dramatic shit, Witter."

I laughed and leaned forward. "But the dramatic shit is the best part and when you hear this, you'll agree."

His gaze narrowed. "Fine. Out with it."

"Having us plan the wedding together and publicly serves another purpose. It will let my sponsors see that I'm the guy they want me to be, they need me to be. Solid and stable, keeping my woman happy."

A slow grin spread across Jack's face and he nodded intensely. "Oh shit Alex, you *are* more than a pretty face."

"I don't hate hearing that."

"Seriously," Jack began. "This isn't just perfect, we'll probably get a few more endorsement deals. Maybe even get a few to pitch in on this wedding." He was practically beaming with cartoon dollar signs in his eyes. "I like it. I like it a lot, but I also don't trust it. I've known you for years Alex and I know when you're up to something. Whatever it is, don't let it screw up everything."

I flashed my signature charming grin and shrugged. "I have no plans to screw anything up." Maybe I had a bad case of having my cake and eating it too, but Sasha was the cake and I wanted it.

I needed it.

Soon enough, I would satisfy my need.

Hell, I would satisfy us both.

"I'm serious. Whatever you do, don't fuck this up man."

I got out of my chair and smiled. "I wouldn't dream of it."

Chapter 18

Sasha

"What am I doing?" I stared at my reflection in the mirror and I barely recognized myself. Like any woman who wanted to enhance her looks, I wore makeup regularly, but usually a bit of shimmery powder, mascara and lip gloss, just enough to look presentable in public. But today I had on eyeshadow, my brows were sculpted to within an inch of their lives and my lips were a gorgeous shade of pink. "I look like one of those yoga moms."

I looked down at my outfit and frowned. Alex had asked me to meet him some place, which meant I had to leave the penthouse, and just outside were dozens of photographers. So I had to dress the part of a woman Alex would ask to marry him. The pale blue sundress had spaghetti straps which made my boobs look even bigger, but the fitted bodice highlighted by hourglass figure and the full skirt stopped at my knees, hiding my thighs. I looked nice, but too dressed up to care for a baby.

But caring for Dixie is my job, so I have to find a way.

"All right, I'm ready." Henrietta appeared in the doorway with a smile and a sparkle in her eye. "Wow, you're going to make Alex swallow his tongue in that dress. Maybe yours too," she laughed.

"Doubtful," I lied easily, shoving memories of his kisses deep down. "what are you ready for?"

"Alex asked me to look after Dixie while you and he *took care of business.*" She added an eyebrow wiggle that said she thought this outing was a ruse.

"What? Why?" The sole reason I was here was for Dixie, and now he was shoving my work onto poor Henrietta. "That's not right."

"It's all right, Sasha. I don't mind. In fact, I'm looking forward to it." She smiled genuinely and my shoulders relaxed. "I'm positive."

"Okay, if you're sure."

"I am, and you look too fine to waste that dress on me and Dixie." She laughed and shook her head before she shooed me out of my bedroom. "Go on and have fun."

I wasn't sure about the fun part, but Alex had asked me to meet him so I grabbed my bag and headed down to the lobby, a pit of anxiety in my belly. I knew what was waiting for me out there and as the elevator doors slid open, I prepared myself for the onslaught.

"You can't go this way, Miss Sasha." Barry's brows

knitted together in confusion. "Your driver, Ben, is waiting in the garage for you."

It was my turn to frown in confusion. "I don't have a driver."

He smiled. "You do now." The gleam in his eyes should have made me feel better, but it didn't.

"I don't need a driver," I told the man I assumed was Ben when the elevator doors opened again.

"Excellent since I'm not a driver. I'm your personal security." His smirk would have amused me if it didn't scare the hell out of me.

"A bodyguard! I don't need a bodyguard."

"Mr. Witter believes otherwise. Are we leaving now?" His dark brows hitched up as he waited for me to answer.

I glanced at the time and growled. "Yeah, okay. Fine." I had about twenty minutes to meet with Alex and I didn't have time to argue with my bodyguard.

"Sorry," I grumbled from the backseat. "I'm Sasha."

He smiled. "I'm Ben. It's nice to meet you, Sasha."

"You too, Ben." It wasn't his fault and I didn't need to take it out on him. We rode in silence for fifteen quiet minutes before I interrupted the silence with a shocked gasp. The building was gorgeous with its wrought iron details and the bell tower above. Bell Tower? I wondered what this place was, but when I spotted Alex outside with a well-dressed woman in head to toe beige, I knew.

"Thanks, Ben."

"Sasha," he called out with a smile, meeting me halfway with a sweet hug, and a kiss that was a lot less sweet with a hell of a lot of heat. "Right on time," he whispered in my ear after breaking the kiss.

"We have an audience," I whispered and nodded towards the group of giddy photographers behind me.

"For a good cause," he promised and pulled back, taking my hand in his as we walked to the woman in beige. "This is Zora, the manager of this venue. What do you think?"

"It's gorgeous. Is that bell tower real?"

Zora nodded. "And working as well."

I listened with half an ear as Zora guided us through the most gorgeous wedding venue I'd ever been inside of. I couldn't focus, couldn't concentrate with Alex's hand in mine. The casual kisses on my hand, the way he brushed a strand of hair from my face, tucking it behind my ear. All of it was wreaking havoc on my mind and my hormones.

It was all too much and I needed to get a grip. This wasn't real, not my relationship with Alex or this wedding. I mean it was real as in it would be legal, but we weren't in love except for the cameras. I pasted on a smile and tugged his big body to a stop, smiling up at him as if he were mine.

"This place is great, babe. But do we have a head count yet? You still haven't sent me your half of the guest list." There, the mundane details of wedding planning should have helped get me back on solid footing, but Alex's smile shot that idea all to hell.

His big hand cupped the side of my face and he slowly brought his mouth down to mine for a slow kiss that incinerated my panties and stole my breath. He pulled back with a slow, sultry grin. "You're right, honey." He looked over at Zora with a sheepish smile. "I guess I got so excited about marrying Sasha that I skipped over some important details, like all the details before the wedding day."

I laughed and bumped him with my hip. "The wedding night, don't you mean?"

Zora laughed and put both hands to her chest. "You two are so adorable," she cooed. "Congratulations." She handed me her business card. "When you get those details settled, give me a call."

I promised I would and let Alex lead me out of the venue with one arm flung lazily around my shoulders as if this was perfectly natural. "That dress is making it hard to focus on anything but your cleavage."

My breath hitched at his whispered words. "Luckily you don't have anything else to focus on," I said and smiled up at him. "Other than why I now have a bodyguard?"

He was still looking at my cleavage and licking his lips. "Yeah, sure."

"Focus," I smiled and snapped my fingers in his face. "Up. Here."

His smile grew. "Jack recommended it and I agreed. You can't focus on the road *and* Dixie while being chased by photographers, that's what Ben is for."

Ugh, that was an excellent point. "Fine. My eyes are still up here."

"Yeah but your cleavage is still down there, and your tits are a thing of beauty." He licked his lips and leaned in, brushing a whisper soft kiss across my lips. "How does dinner sound?"

"Like this, arrghrrhrh."

He froze, smiled wide, and then broke out into a laugh so loud and so masculine that it was contagious and we stood on the sidewalk laughing together like we were completely alone.

It was the kind of moment that made a girl forget what was real and what was fake.

Chapter 19

Alex

"I should have taken you to one of those seafood restaurants that hand out bibs." Sasha's cleavage was so fucking distracting that we'd been sitting at our table for fifteen minutes and I still hadn't even picked up the menu.

Her lips spread into a gorgeous grin and her head fell back as she laughed. "Sorry?"

My lips pursed through my smile and I leaned forward, gaze fixed on hers. Finally. "Oh, I think you know what I mean."

She kept laughing until her laughter faded. "I needed to look presentable in front of the cameras, like a woman you would be with." She looked down nervously, and for the first time I understood what all of this must be like for Sasha. She was nothing like Tatiana who always dressed to be photographed because that was her goal in life, to be seen.

"Well you knocked it out of the park, because right now all I want is to be with you Sasha." It wasn't a line either, she'd been on my mind all day, through my training and practice sessions, and even the shower. Especially in the shower

Her smile dimmed and she pointed at me. "No. We talked about this."

"Talked, yes. But we didn't agree to anything." In fact I was putting my thumb on the scale by making reservations at this romantic hotspot where we could be seen, but it also offered enough privacy for the romance portion of the evening.

She rolled her eyes at me but an affectionate smile stayed on her lush mouth. "How was the first day of practice?"

I stared at her like she was an alien, stunned by her question. When was the last time a woman had asked me about work? The answer was simple, never. Other than my mother, no woman ever asked. They want to know about my teammates, my endorsement deals and the things my lifestyle affords me, but never the thing that gave me that lifestyle.

Sasha's brows knitted at my silence and sat back. "Sorry. Is that too personal?" Her shoulders slumped forward. "I thought we were getting to know…never mind. Forget I asked."

"No," I reached out and covered her hand with mine, swiping my back and forth across her wrist. "It's not too personal at all, I'm just surprised at the question.

I can't remember the last time someone asked me about work."

She nodded, easily accepting my answer. "Well?"

My lips curled up and I relaxed back into my seat. "It was good to be back. I've been training hard to get ready for the season and I'm glad for it, these new guys are dying to take my place on the roster."

"You're not even thirty yet."

"And some of my teammates are barely twenty." A fact that became more obvious with each passing day.

"Okay, so they're younger. What do you have that makes you the best winger in the league?"

"Someone's been doing her homework."

"I have," she admitted. "But not even Google can make me understand what your job actually is."

"On offense, I find or create space to pass the puck, intercept passes from the other team and attack whoever has the puck."

"So you're a jack of all trades?"

"Kind of, yeah." I was so excited talking to a beautiful woman about hockey that again, I forgot to look at the menu. Only this time it wasn't her tits that had my attention, at least not all of it.

"Are we ready to order?"

I looked up at the server and suddenly I knew exactly what Sasha meant about starting to care because dammit, now I was starting to care about more than getting her in bed. "Um, yeah," I replied and ordered the ravioli.

Sasha placed her order before she turned those

sparkling blue eyes back to me. "So, jack of all trades on the ice?"

I nodded but now it felt different, too intimate to talk about the game I loved with her. "We should probably focus on wedding talk for a while."

Confusion flashed but she concealed it quickly and sat back, putting physical as well as emotional distance between us. "Oh. Right. The wedding is why we're here." She shook off *something* and when her gaze met mine again, it was distant and wary. "I'll invite some of my friends from the agency since I don't keep in touch with my so-called friends from school."

"And your parents?"

She shrugged. "I'd rather not invite them but doing that would only invite more questions than if they showed up so I guess put them on the list." As if just realizing something, she pulled out her phone and tapped the screen a few times. "I've started the guest list and I'll share it with you or Jack, and you can add to it as necessary."

"Oh, um, yeah that sounds good." The mood at the table had shifted abruptly and it was my fault. "This is weird."

She shrugged and turned to her wine. "It's happening," she whispered and kept her gaze focused on the empty plate in front of her. "Maybe we should just take the food to go, let them think we couldn't wait until after dinner to ravish each other." There was no emotion, no fire in her words and I wanted to kick myself.

"Oh my god, Alex Witter!" A group of guys stopped at

the table, all smiles and handshakes, as they asked for a selfie and told me how great I was. It never got old, that was for sure.

"This is my fiancé, Sasha."

She smiled sweetly and four sets of eyes swung to her and widened. "Hey guys."

"Damn, that's her? Good for you, Alex."

"What did you expect," another guy asked. "A stick like Tatiana? Nah, Witter wants a real woman."

"Uh, guys?"

"Oh sorry!" They apologized for the intrusion, thanked me and went on their way.

"You love it," she said with an affectionate smile. And then, as if she remembered we weren't being friendly, it faded and she went back to her wine.

"I do. Without the fans I wouldn't be who I am. Sure, I'd still play and I would still be damn good but without the love, I wouldn't make what I do or have the endorsements that fund my lifestyle."

She nodded. "Then it's good that you enjoy it." That was it, her words bland and stilted.

The rest of dinner was excruciating and I wasn't sure which I preferred, falling under her spell or having her ice me out completely.

By the time we made it back to the penthouse, I had my answer. I would much rather—a million times over—fall under Sasha's spell than be the subject of her cold shoulder. She hadn't said a word since she argued with me about paying half the dinner tab at the restaurant, which made for a torturous ride home.

"Where are you going?" She looked up at me as we made a left down the hall that led to her suite.

"I'm walking you to your door," I told her. "Like a gentleman."

Sasha sighed. "You don't have to do this, Alex. We tried tonight and we failed, so let's just chalk it up to giving it the old college try, okay?"

"I wouldn't say we failed," I began slowly and put my hand to her lower back, where I didn't fail to miss the shiver that tore through her body. "There are learning curves to be expected."

"Learning curves?" She laughed but there was a distinct lack of amusement in it. "I tried to get to know you and you shut me down. Message received." She turned at the door and effectively blocked me from going any further. "Good night, Alex."

Shit. This was not going the way I wanted it to go, and I hated it. This wasn't me. Alex Witter didn't swing his puck and miss, not ever. I always made the goal. Except tonight. I watched Sasha turn away with slumped shoulders and a defeated expression and knew I had to do something. "I finally understand now, what you were trying to tell me before."

She stopped and turned to me, her dark brows raised in a question.

"The dangers of spending time together. The risk of catching inconvenient feelings." I shook my head and scraped a hand over my face. "I felt it earlier and it shocked me, not because you're not great but because, hell Sasha, you asked me about work. Do you know how fucking hot that is?"

She shook her head. "I have no idea Alex. We're going to be spending a lot of time together over the next two and a half years, I thought it would be nice to get to know each other."

"I want that too," I insisted. "It just dawned on me during dinner what you meant and I could see how easily feelings could develop."

"And you either hated it or got scared," she guessed correctly.

"It scared me, Sasha. It scared the hell out of me." My lips pulled into a lopsided grin but the minute it was over, I hated the way you pulled back. I hated it more than it scared me."

"I get it, Alex. Now you understand why this is a bad deal."

"I understand why *you* think it's a bad idea," I agreed and took a step forward. And then another. "But I disagree." She got as far as a gasp before my mouth was on hers, tasting the white wine on her lips from dinner, the after dinner coffee on her tongue. I smiled against her mouth and she moaned when I slipped inside. She moaned again when I pulled her close to let her feel the impact she had on me.

Sasha and I were good together, really fucking good and this kiss proved it. All it took was one swipe of my tongue, one nibble on my bottom lip and we both blew up. It was explosive and there was no way in hell that we could spend the next two and a half years together without getting naked. Together.

In fact, if I didn't stop now then I'd peel that blue dress off of her and make her scream my name now. *Pull back now.* After a few more seconds of devouring every inch of her mouth, I slowly pulled back with a teasing grin. "As much as I want to, and I really fucking want to, I don't put out on the first date."

She laughed. "Who's offering?"

I laughed and leaned in, kissing the top of one breast and then the other. The kiss was silky smooth and she smelled like flowers and perfume. "Not yet, Sasha. But soon."

Very fucking soon.

I stepped back until she was out of my reach and then I turned and walked away, and straight into a cold shower.

Chapter 20

Sasha

T*his cannot continue.* How many nights was this man, this frustrating beautiful man, going to invade my dreams? It was unfair really, the way he'd kissed me after he'd been so wishy-washy on what was so far our first—and only—date. How could a man be so unsure of his feelings yet kiss like I meant everything to him? It was magic or maybe sorcery, it was some sort of supernatural bullshit.

Instead of lying in bed while my mind played and replayed that kiss, heating up the blood as it pumped through my veins and dampening my panties, I sat up abruptly and jumped out of bed. I couldn't start another day with Alex on my mind, even if he was my husband-to-be. No, I dressed quickly and check on Dixie, who was thankfully awake and ready to start the day. "You're a lifesaver, pretty girl."

At the sound of my voice Dixie smiled, a sight that

never failed to make my chest squeeze just a little. She was a sweet baby in need of love and I was happy to lavish her with it.

"At least you're happy to see me." Unlike her father who had spent most of the past week avoiding me. If I walked into a room, he left that room. He made sure not to touch me when he took over to spend time with Dixie. And most of all, we hadn't been on a second date. We hadn't had any more heart-pounding kisses.

The thing was, I missed Alex. Sure he was arrogant and too charming by half, and he knew his worth as a man, but he was also funny and kind. He smelled like a man should and yeah okay, maybe I also missed the way his body felt under my hands. Hard and sculpted, rippling and so hot that my hands tingled just thinking about touching him.

"Damn," I whispered under my breath and forbid myself from having any more Alex related thoughts until the sun set hours from now.

So far so good. I hadn't thought of him once while I dressed Dixie for the day, or when I ventured outside of her room and into the kitchen. Twenty minutes and then forty-five minutes passed and I hadn't thought of him once.

And then there he was, appearing out of nowhere in a pair of shorts that hung low—mouthwateringly low—on his hips, and no shirt because the man had an aversion to wearing too many clothes. "Good morning, ladies." He flashed a toothy grin and I turned away, kept my focus on feeding Dixie.

Henrietta turned and gave him a long, assessing look before she frowned at him. "Something wrong with your shirts?"

"It's summer," he reminded her as if that was a full answer or an answer period.

Henrietta pointed her wooden spoon at him and then the vents hidden on the walls. "There's air conditioning in here."

I laughed and continued feeding Dixie who was having a full blown baby conversation on her own.

Alex crossed the kitchen and stopped in front of me, his gaze focused on me while I staunchly avoided his gaze. He plucked Dixie from the high chair. "Mornin' sweet girl." My heart kicked up at the sight of father and daughter smiling at each other with adoration. He smacked a loud kiss to her cheek that made her face split with a sweet smile. "What do you think about hanging out with your Dad today?"

No, no, no. Going to the park would involve me and it was likely also involve the press and I wasn't in the mood. "Don't you have practice?" I stood purposefully and offered Dixie another spoonful of roasted summer squash.

"Nope. Some kind of management meeting so we have a free day and I was thinking we could go to the park together. All three of us." His green eyes were so full of hope that I wanted to say yes immediately, but I couldn't. Not yet.

Instantly my gaze was wary as it darted all around the kitchen, everywhere but at Alex and his hopeful expression. I had no good reason to say no and since the contract had already been sighed, I couldn't technically say no. Instead I thought about a few tips to help me keep my emotional distance from a man like Alex. He was entirely too potent, took up to much space in every room he was in, and most of all, he was irresistible. There was no other answer I could give so I shrugged inwardly and agreed. "Yeah, sure. We can go to the park. It'll be fun for Dixie." My smile felt phony which was good because it was, things were too awkward now and I didn't like it, knew I couldn't deal with two years of that problem.

"Great. We can leave in an hour if that works for you?"

I nodded and finished feeding Dixie, knowing I had one hour of peace before I had to touch Alex, accept his affection and return it. All for show.

I had sixty minutes to get my head screwed on straight and ready to pretend for the cameras.

Only for the cameras.

Seventy-five minutes later Alex and I strolled through the park with our hands clasped, Dixie strapped to his chest as she smiled and babbled at everything in sight. Her eyes lit with excitement at the colors of the flowers, the dogs and kids. The sounds.

His hand squeezed mine and I looked up into those eyes, sparkling with joy. "You think she's enjoying herself?"

I smiled softly at the concern in his question and nodded. "Hang on." I held a hand up to stop him and rushed forward with my phone in my hand, snapping a few photos. "Okay, now walk."

His brows knitted together at the command but a moment later he started walking again and Dixie's face lit up even more. I let the video record for a few seconds and tapped the stop button. "What was that?"

I shrugged. "I wanted to put your mind at ease." I returned to Alex's side and showed him the photos and then the video. My goodness he was as gorgeous as they made men and when a soft smile touched his lips, my attraction only intensified.

"She's smiling!"

"She likes being out here in the world, seeing the sights and sounds, don't ya, Dix?"

"Thanks," he mumbled. The moment was ruined by the sound of cameras clicking but Alex's smile only brightened as he leaned forward and pressed a too hot and too damn short kiss against my lips.

"You're welcome," I whispered, my voice low and breathy.

"Wipe that look off your face or I won't be responsible for what happens next," he growled, his gaze dark with desire.

I blinked and shook my head. "What are you talking about? What look?"

Alex leaned forward and whispered in my ear. "That

look that says you want me to devour you whole. I will, Sasha. Just say the word."

The word. What word would that be? *Yes, please, have your wicked way with me?* I wanted that, so bad I could taste it, but I couldn't. Not with this man and not now. "We, uh, shouldn't complicate things Alex."

He tossed his head back and laughed. "Things are already pretty damn complicated Sasha. What isn't, is how much I want you."

"Dammit," I muttered and cast a look over my shoulder at the photographers not even pretending to keep a respectful distance from us as they snapped more photos than they could ever possibly sell.

He laughed again before taking my hand and continuing our stroll through the park. His hand was so hot, so big and strong that I found it difficult to concentrate on anything else.

"Do you get a chance to get out like this often without the cameras?"

He laughed but there was no humor in it. "I wish. When I went to visit Dante recently it was nice, it's easier to relax outside the city without photographers. It was nice too, a lot of high-fives and congratulations but not a lot of autographs and photos. It was...nice." He sighed the last word and in that moment I empathized with him.

"That must be hard."

Alex nodded. "I suspect its why the pay is so damn good."

I frowned. "To make up for the lack of privacy?"

"No," he laughed. "To turn your home into all the things you can't do in public without interruption. To fly in a private jet so you can just sleep or read a book. Things like that."

I smiled up at him, impressed with his ability to make light of a pretty serious invasion of privacy. "That's a good way of looking at it."

"You think?"

I nodded. "I do. You could be bitter about it, or you could be like those celebrities you hear about who are secretly awful. You grin and bear it publicly and find ways to enjoy your life outside the public eye."

"Sounds like you might be impressed."

"I am," I shrugged. "It takes a lot of strength to deal with this," I motioned to the gang of people following us, "and not get angry as hell about it." I looked up and our gazes locked for a long, hot moment. His gaze was as hot as my skin felt and it had nothing to do with the Texas sun. I couldn't look away and I didn't want to, at least not until the telltale camera click ruined the moment.

Again.

Thankfully.

Soon enough Dixie dozed off and I knew it was time to head back to the penthouse. I rubbed the soft tendrils that peeked out from under her hat and smiled. "Time to head back home."

"So soon?"

I flashed a smile as I nodded. "You're the one who

didn't want to bring her stroller and we can't let her head bob around like that. So, ready?"

"Yeah, sure."

Was that disappointment I heard in his voice? Maybe he was just missing being outside with the sun and without the bother. Yes, that had to be it. I brushed off my own disappointment as we turned towards the photographers, who parted for us though they never stopped snapping photos and made our way out of the park.

Once inside the penthouse, my shoulders finally relaxed. My heart though, raced as Alex's nearness and the heat of his body swirled around me. I focused on taking Dixie's sleeping body from the baby carrier, not on his broad chest or masculine scent. "I'll just put her down for her afternoon nap." Then, like the coward I was, I rushed away and then I hid in my room like any sane woman would.

I kicked off my sandals and flopped down on the plush bed with a sigh. And a smile. It was nice to get out of the penthouse for awhile without running errands. The photographers weren't great but the day was still nice and Dixie seemed to love it.

A knock sounded so soft I wasn't sure if I was hearing things or not, until another knock came. My heart raced as I answered the door knowing that Henrietta was out shopping, which meant my visitor could just be one person. I opened the door and Alex stood there with a shy smile on his face unlike any of his other smiles. "Alex."

"Sasha."

We stared at each other the same way we had earlier only now it was more charged, so heated the electricity crackled between us. "What's up?"

"I, uh, I had a good time today. Thanks for agreeing to it."

"So did I and I'm pretty sure Dixie had the most fun." My lips parted into a playful smile. "And the photographers were only mildly annoying."

His brow quirked. "Already getting used to the limelight?"

"Hardly," I huffed out a laugh. "But that controlled chaos was better than being bombarded when you're least expecting it."

"Yeah," he sighed, his big green eyes focused on my mouth.

My tongue slid out and swept across my lips, suddenly breathless at the hungry way he looked at me. "Alex." His name came out on a shaky whisper and I took a step back.

He stepped forward. "Sasha." He growled my name and hooked an arm around my waist, pulling me so our bodies were flush together. "Tell me to stop." His words were a plea and as much as I wanted to say those exact words, I couldn't.

"I can't."

Alex didn't say another word, he just smashed his mouth against mine, kissing me like the world would end if he didn't. His lips were firm and demanding, his tongue slipped between my lips and when I gasped, he tilted my head back and deepened the kiss.

I growled and tangled my fingers in his thick blond hair, pulling him closer. Alex kissed the same way he did everything else, with an intense focus that explained exactly why he was so successful.

His hands slid up the outside of my thighs and I'd never been so grateful for a sundress in my life. The feel of his slightly roughened hands against my skin was intoxicating and I arched into him, tugged his hair a little harder. He pulled back and stared at me with glossy eyes. "Sasha."

I smiled as his hand slid between my thighs, his thumb found my clit over the scrap of damp cotton that covered me. "Fuck," I moaned.

"Exactly." With one quick move, the dress was off my body and sailing to the floor.

This was happening.

Holy shit this was happening.

Chapter 21

Alex

"You are so fucking beautiful," I murmured as I laid Sasha across her bed and took in the sight of her, all womanly curves and silky skin, chest heaving beneath the pale pink bra. "And you were hiding all of this under that sexy little dress?"

She bit her bottom lip and nodded. "Not hiding, most of us don't walk around half naked all day."

I laughed but my nostrils flared at her sassy words. "If I'd known I would have put a condition in the contract that you walk around naked most of the time."

Sasha rolled her eyes. "You don't have to say that, Alex."

"I don't say things I don't mean, Sasha. You're beautiful, accept it." I trailed my fingertips up and down her skin, across her belly and the inside of her thighs, enjoying the way she shivered at my touch. "And if you don't accept it," I pressed a kiss just above the waistband of her panties. "Then I'll just have to make you believe that I want you."

"Oh god," she groaned and I smiled against her, hooking my thumbs through her panties and sliding them down her legs. "Alex."

"That's exactly what I want to hear, you crying my name as I make you come."

Her breath hitched at my words. I removed her bra and the sight of her stole my breath again. "You gonna stare or you gonna act, Winger?"

Oh shit, a naked woman talking hockey? I didn't think my cock could get harder. "First of all, I'm gonna do both."

She smiled sweetly but the pulse in her throat beat wildly, another sure sign she was as turned on as I was. "That sounds like a good place to start."

I chuckled at her playfulness and used my shoulders to part her thighs, the sweet scent of her arousal hit my nose and my cock stiffened, aching with my need to have her. To make her mine. "Then let's start, shall we?" I didn't give her a chance to speak before my hands gripped her thighs and held her open while I devoured her. She was pink and wet, and the taste of her was pure fucking magic.

"Alex," she moaned, the sound deep and guttural. Hot as fuck. Her body trembled when my tongue flicked out, sliding against her bare lips before I parted her open and tortured her clit for long minutes. "Oh. My. God."

Damn straight. I devoured Sasha whole, licking and sucking her sweet pussy while she moaned and writhed beneath me. The sound of my name as it fell from her lips over and over, riled me up and I slid one finger and then two fingers deep and crooked my finger. She arched into me, gripping my hair tight as pleasure flooded her veins, incoherent words fell from her lips as her body quivered with her orgasm.

"Fuck, Alex."

I looked up with a smile. "That's next, sweetheart." My cock ached to get inside her and I sat up on my knees, staring down at her. "You ready for me?"

Instead of answering, Sasha shoved me away and got to her knees so we were nearly face to face. "Beyond ready," she growled and quickly relieved me of every stitch of clothing I had on, kissing all the hard flesh she uncovered. "You are so gorgeous," she growled and pushed me backwards until my head hung over the foot of the bed.

My cock was impossibly hard as she kissed my pecs, my abs down to the vee at my hips where her tongue traced down one way and up the other. "Ah, fuck. Sasha, babe." She was torturing me and I was completely at her mercy as one soft hand gripped my cock, stroking long and hard.

She sat up and looked at me with a smile. "You're big and hard everywhere."

My jaw clamped down hard to slow the pressure she gave easily. "Sasha," I growled and reached for her but she was just out of my grasp. "Fuck," I grunted as my hips bucked up at the feel of her tongue slicing across my slit. And then, sweet heavens above, my cock was in her mouth. Hot and wet and oh so fucking capable, I was powerless to do anything but go with it.

She moaned, gripping me tight as she took me deeper and deeper, still moaning as if she was enjoying it as much as I was. Finally she took me to the back of her throat and moaned again.

My balls tightened and I grabbed a handful of black hair. "You're going to kill me," I growled as I laid her down and spread my body over hers.

"Oh, but what a way to go."

I smiled, covering my mouth with hers as I slid deep. She was hot and wet and ready for me, thank fuck, because my control was at the end of its rope. "Fuck," I bit out and looked down at Sasha. She was the most beautiful thing I'd ever seen with her black hair splayed out across the pillows, her eyes fluttered shut and her teeth pressed into her bottom lip, the column of her throat exposed to me. I licked a trail of heat from the hollow in her throat and back up to her mouth.

"You're the devil," she moaned as she tightened around me in a series of lightning quick pulses.

"Even the devil can be tempted, sweetheart." She tempted me beyond all reason and the worst part was that I didn't give a damn. I had Sasha right where I wanted her and I wasn't anywhere near done with her.

"Alex," she panted, her hands gripped my biceps and her ankles locked behind my back. She bucked up at the same time I slammed deep again and that was all she needed to fall apart. "Oh fuck," she moaned in my ear. "Yes, Alex. Yes!"

That was exactly what every man longed to hear when he was pleasing his woman, the sounds of her pleasure, of her begging for more. I sat back and watched as she rode the wave of her orgasm with a sexy as fuck smile on her face. My cock tightened inside of her and I couldn't wait another minute. "I'll lock that image away for later," I told her and yanked her closer, tossing her legs over my thighs, her round ass cupped in my hand to change the angle.

Sasha pulsed around me and the harder and deeper I pounded into her, the longer her orgasm was drawn out. I pulled a hard nipple between my lips, sucking and nibbling as I chased down my orgasm. When it hit, it was explosive, it was powerful, it was all-consuming. It was unlike any orgasm of my life and I never wanted it to end. "Alex," she cried out as another, more powerful orgasm slammed into her, ultimately triggering my own.

"Ah, fuck Sasha! Yes!" My body jerked and shook as pleasure seeped out of me and into her body. Every inch of me coiled tight until it exploded with shards of light, bursts of need, a pleasure bomb. "Sasha." I shook and fell over her so we were chest to chest, face to face.

She opened her mouth to say something but I couldn't say what because Dixie was awake and screaming for attention. Sasha opened her mouth and then snapped it shut two or three times before she shoved me off her.

I rolled her and watched her as she scrambled off the bed, shoving her arms through my t-shirt and headed for the adjoining door. She turned to me with something in her eyes I couldn't quite decipher, and then she disappeared into Dixie's room.

I wasn't sure if I was relieved or disappointed.

All I knew was that already I was hungry to have her again.

And again.

I woke up the next morning hard and aching, thoughts of Sasha dancing in my mind while visions of her luscious curves played behind my eyelids. She was so soft everywhere, with a small waist, meaty tits and thick thighs that felt warm and snug wrapped around me. Her scent still surrounded me because I hadn't bothered to shower after leaving her room because I wasn't ready to wash away our time together.

I grunted, annoyed that I hadn't bothered to wash away her scent because now it tortured me. It reminded me of her, of the way she looked and sounded as I thrust into her, the way she gripped my hair tight when I made her feel good. My hand slipped under the sheet and fisted my cock, almost like it had a mind of its own.

I go with it, leaning back against the pillows with my eyes closed, gripping my cock, stroking it roughly to thoughts of Sasha. The way she took my cock down her throat without being asked, and then moaned as if she liked it. "Fuck," I groaned and stroked faster. Harder.

Even now the scent and the sound of her was so visceral it was like she was here, on top of me. Like it was her wet pussy instead of my hand, gripping me tight and bringing me closer to the edge. I stroke and stroke with just one thought on my mind.

I want more.

No, fuck that, I need more.

More Sasha.

Now.

I was so close to starting my day off with a Sasha induced orgasm when my door smacked open and my agent and sometimes friend, Jack, appeared in the doorway. Though right now I was sure he was nothing more than my enemy. "What the fuck, Jack?"

His gaze landed on me, a smirk on his face like he knew exactly what I was doing and who I was thinking about while I did it. "We need to move the wedding up. ASAP."

My hand fell from my cock and I sat up, brows knitted into a deep frown. "Why, what happened?"

"Nothing bad for once." His shoulders relaxed and he looked around my room before dropping down into the chair beside the door. "I spoke to reps from Johnson Athletics and St. Bay Lager, both of which are interested in paying you a fat sum to use that pretty face to sell their goods. If your profile stays high right now, we can probably get this signed in the next fourteen days. You up for that?"

Johnson Athletics was the dream for any pro athlete. And beer? Well, beer was always a good bet for hockey fans and puck bunnies, not that I had any interest in them with or without a wife. "Yeah, I'm up for it."

"Good." Jack stood and kicked the sturdy bed frame with a wide grin. "Get your pretty ass out of bed, toss some water on your face and get your bride-to-be. We've got work to do."

My ears and my cock perked up at his mention of Sasha. "I'll be out in five."

"Make it ten. I need you extra pretty to get Sasha on board." Jack smiled and then disappeared, probably to go bother Henrietta.

When I entered the kitchen, Sasha was there with a wide-eyed look on her face while Jack prattled on, probably about the need for an expedited wedding. "Help," she mouthed when Jack turned to me with a smile.

"You started without me," I said as I walked across the kitchen to get a cup of hot, black coffee, turning my gaze to Sasha.

"I did," Jack said, completely unbothered by Sasha's shocked look. "But I see you're dressed for the job at hand, so I'll let you do the honors."

"Yeah, okay." I slowly sipped my coffee as I crossed the kitchen and dropped down at the head of the table. "The good news is that neither of us will have to endure six months of wedding planning."

Her gaze didn't move, didn't waver for a long moment and I braced for the worst. Instead I was met with the sweet and husky sound of her laughter. "Sold, how long do we have?"

"July is a great month for a wedding," Jack said, attempting to sound innocent.

Sasha frowned. "Won't everyone think I'm pregnant if we get married so soon?"

I shrugged. "It won't hurt for people to know I'm young and virile."

She rolled her eyes but she couldn't hide the smirk that curled her lips. "Fine. A day in July." She folded her arms in resignation and looked at me expectantly.

"How about a Friday," Jack asked in that way that wasn't really asking. "You can have a long weekend away together and then later you can do a big honeymoon. We'll make a big splash out of it." He smiled, all self-satisfied.

"Sounds like you want to moonlight as a wedding planner," Sasha told him with a sassy smile.

Jack flashed a wide smile as a laugh escaped. "No can do, sweetheart. That part is up to you two and try to make it splashy if you can." His gaze settled on Sasha, appraising her or maybe just her appearance. "Don't forget to dress up for the cameras. Play up those curves." He wiggled his eyebrows.

"Watch it," Sasha aimed a finger at him. "If you die another agent will step in to take your place."

Her words startled a laugh out of me and Henrietta.

"Noted," Jack said and pushed away from the table. "Keep me posted. Later, Henrietta."

I turned to Sasha with a resigned smile though I was secretly happy that we had a reason to spend the whole day together. "How long do you need to get ready?"

"I have a job," she shot back.

"I'll take care of the little one," Henrietta offered. "It's better than cleaning anyway. She smells better than your dirty socks," she said with a playful smile aimed at me.

She arched a brow at me, a sassy expression on her face. "An hour will suffice."

"Perfect. Wear something pretty for me."

Sasha glared at me as she pushed away from the table, flipping me the bird as she left the kitchen.

"I hope you know what you're doing," Henrietta said behind me.

"So do I." The truth was that now that I've had Sasha, I wanted her even more than ever. In my bed, but also in my life.

"Just try not to screw it up."

I sighed and turned to my housekeeper. "I'll try my best."

She smiled down at me. "Then it's as good as done."

Henrietta's faith in me was what gave me the confidence to move forward. She knew about my screwups in the early days of my career and she'd stuck around, giving me tough love and motherly affection. She knew what I could do and the fact that she thought I could do this and not screw it up, hell it meant that I could.

That I would.

Chapter 22

Sasha

My shoulders sagged as we checked out the fifth venue in four hours. They were all gorgeous venues, with curling staircases, vibrant gardens, bell towers, archways, gazebos and anything else that a little girl might dream up for her wedding day. They were stunning and they were overpriced, which wasn't a problem for Alex. But there was another problem with each and every single venue. "It's too much for a small wedding."

Alex kept his hand closed around mine, nodding his agreement. "They are all great, Diana, but my lovely bride is right, it's too much for an intimate ceremony."

The woman gave a tight-lipped smile, disappointed that she wouldn't be responsible for throwing a wedding for one of the biggest athletes in the country. "I'm sorry to hear that, but we have a sister site that might suit you." She handed me a business card and offered a smile for Alex. "Good luck. And congratulations."

Jack was a bit of an overbearing ass, but I was grateful to him for suggesting we move the wedding forward. It was exhausting and we were only a few hours into planning a fake wedding. "How about we just stop at the courthouse on our way back to the penthouse?"

He sighed and pressed a kiss to the back of my hand. "We'd still have to wait seventy-two hours." He led me out of the venue and into the waiting car, stopping just long enough to smile for the cameras. "Besides it'll look like I'm ashamed of you or like you said, that we have something to hide."

Fair enough. "Then how about we find a place that can accommodate about fifty or so guests and that can do a wedding and reception in one place? Less planning for us." We had exactly one month to put together a wedding fit for a hockey star.

His eyes lit up. "I know just the place. I used to stay at the Andromeda when I came to visit Dante so the photographers wouldn't camp out at his place and frighten Lena." Excitement lit his eyes and highlighted his stunning good looks, so fine I had to look away. "Damn near every time I stayed, there was a wedding happening."

"Okay. Let's go there." I was hopeful that this place would be everything we needed because I was tired and bored, and most of all I didn't want to waste a wedding venue I might want to use one day for a real wedding.

A real marriage.

Two hours later we didn't just have a wedding venue and a reception hall—all in one place, thank you very much—but it was booked and the deposit was paid. It was done. Alex and I were getting married. "It's not too late to back out," I teased.

"Don't even think about it, sweetheart. You're wearing my ring. You're mine." The intensity in his gaze startled me, it stole my breath.

In that moment I realized that I wanted it to be real. Shit that was bad. Really bad. "That means you're mine, Winger."

His gaze heated when I said that, the same way they heated the last time I called him that. "Keep it up and we'll really give them something to photograph." Alex wiggled his brows, mouth split into a heart-stopping smile that sent fire rushing through my veins. "In fact," he said with a devilish glint in his green eyes. "Let's do that." And then he pulled me close, kissing the hell out of me, devouring my mouth while at least a dozen cameras snapped our image and who knows how many phone cameras.

I didn't care. I wrapped my arms around him and accepted his masterful kiss like it was my birthright. I don't know how long we stood there in the lobby of the famed Andromeda Hotel, kissing like two people really in love, like two people who couldn't get enough of each other. I breathed in his scent and savored the feel of his body pressed up against mine, the way his hands grazed up and down my back like he was trying to decide whether or not to grab my ass.

Alex pulled back, breathless and smiling. "Let's get out of here."

Yes, please. "Where are we going?"

"To celebrate."

It wasn't what I wanted to hear but after what happened yesterday, I was glad one of us had our head screwed on straight. We still hadn't talked about what happened between us yesterday, as in the mind-altering, axis-tilting, heart-stopping sex—and it looked like Alex had no desire to talk about it. Which was fine. Really, it was fine.

I just needed to push it all out of my head. To stop thinking about Alex in all his naked glory, the way he felt sliding into my body, the intensity and the vigor with which he gave me orgasms. *Stop! No!* I wasn't thinking about it and I wasn't thinking about him.

Period.

I was still *not* thinking about Alex or his bronzed skin and tempting smile two days later as I combed through wedding invitations. The invitations made this real and as I looked through card weights, script types and RSVP cards, this all suddenly become very real. Or *more* real, I suppose. The weight of what we were doing settled all around me, which helped me keep my mind off Alex. Off sex with Alex.

Unfortunately thinking about Alex naked and growling my name like he couldn't get enough of me was preferable to thinking about inviting my parents to the wedding. Mom would be hurt that I didn't tell her I was dating anyone, and more so that I didn't let her help me plan the wedding. And my dad, well he probably wasn't sober enough to care either way.

It didn't matter to me, not really. My father hadn't been an active part of my life for most of my life, but they would both be invited or it might reflect badly on Alex and that would defeat the whole purpose of this charade.

Dixie babbled beside me as I picked three invitations for Alex to approve even though he probably won't care. "What do you think, baby girl?"

Her gummy smile was brilliant as she gave me her answer, incoherent as it was.

"Cool. Let's hope your dad thinks so too." My shoulders fell in disappointment. My feelings were becoming complicated and Alex and I weren't even married yet. I needed to get a damn grip, to shove whatever I thought I was feeling down deep until it was forgotten.

The sound of my phone ringing pulled me from thoughts of my husband-to-be and my complicated feelings, and to the present and another set of complicated feelings. "Hey Mom."

"Sasha, how are you?"

"Good, Mom. How are things?" I let out a silent sigh, wishing our conversations were less stilted and more along mother-daughter lines.

"Good," she sighed. "Always good. Are you still working?"

"I am." Why was this so hard? "I'm glad you called because I have some news. I'm getting married." A long silence descended and I held my breath waiting for a derisive or disappointed comment, but none came. "Mom?"

"I'm here, Sasha. I'm just trying to figure out when you started dating someone and why is this the first I'm hearing of it, when it seems all of the entertainment industry already knows."

Because you made your choice and it wasn't me. "You know why, Mom. I'm telling you now."

"Are you pregnant?"

"No, Mom. I'm not pregnant. Listen, come if you want. I'll send you an invitation."

"Do you want us there?"

I let out a bitter laugh. "That's never been the issue, Mom and you know it. I always want you there but you made your choice every time. Come if you want, Mom. It would be great to see you."

"It would be great to see you too. I miss you, Sasha."

"I miss you too, Mom." But it was her choice to stay with my father after everything so this is what our relationship was reduced too. "I hope you come." But I wouldn't hold my breath. "I need to get back to work, Mom. Love you." I ended the call before she tried to bring my father into the conversation again.

Dixie grunted which meant it was time for a diaper change and it was a sad state of affairs when that was a better option than talking to my mother. I realized what a horrible thought that was considering that Dixie may never see her mother again.

The front door opened and closed and my stupid belly flipped knowing that Alex was home. *Down girl, none of this is real.* Okay, the orgasms were real but those didn't count. They didn't come with love and affection, they were just physical urges. This was for his career, his image and for something that Jack had called his Q Score. This wasn't about me, I was just convenient.

As always, my mere existence was convenient. For my parents and now for my fiancé. I needed to remember that.

"Hey, how are my girls?" Alex flashed a brilliant smile as he leaned against the door in the nursery.

"Good. Productive day at the rink?"

He shrugged. "Pretty good. You?"

"Fine," I sighed. "I have three options for you to choose from for invitations."

"Excellent," his smile brightened and my heart leapt in my chest. "Thank you for taking care of that."

"What are fiancées for if not wedding planning duties?" I picked up Dixie and handed her to Alex since she was reaching for him anyway. It was a good thing that she recognized his face and his voice, that she knew he was someone she could rely on because he was all she really had.

"Hey Dixie, you smell good." He kissed her cheek and smiled affectionately at her and it was so damn cute I had no choice but to look away.

"Excuse me," I murmured and slipped past father and

daughter to give them some privacy. That was a lie, I needed a moment to get myself together. I couldn't waste time nursing this crush on my boss and future husband, not when it wasn't returned and definitely not when it could never be anything more than whatever it was at this moment.

That's enough, I told myself. Alex was nice to look at, he was kind and this would be an easy two years of marriage.

Mostly.

"Hey, Sash," Alex called out and I couldn't stop the shiver at his use of the nickname he'd made up. "These invitations look great. All of them."

I met him in the living room where the laptop with the invitations filled the screen. "All you have to do is choose one."

He glanced at the screen, giving each one a solid fifteen seconds of thought before he moved on to the next. His smile grew and he went back to the second choice. "This one."

My favorite one too. "I'll send it to the printers now so we should have them sometime tomorrow." My eyes darted around the living room in search of something else —anything else—to look at other than his gorgeous smile. "One more thing done," I said as my gaze darted around. "Only about a thousand more to go."

Alex laughed and set Dixie in her swing. "We're almost done. Just a few more things to go and a month from tomorrow we'll be married and this will all be a distant memory."

"I admire your optimism."

His smile brightened. "Thanks." Alex took a step forward and then another. To the outside observer he resembled a predator as he slowly stalked his prey—me—who was powerless to outrun him or his advances. "What else do you admire?"

I laughed and gave his chest a shove but he wrapped one hand around my wrist and pulled me close. "Need your ego stroked, Alex?"

His smile was slow and fiery like a smoldering fire with a magnetic core that pulled me in. "It's not my ego that needs stroking, Sash."

My head fell back and I laughed and in the next second, one hand cupped the back of my head and then his mouth crashed down on mine, his tongue swept across my lips in a drugging back and forth motion that sent fire pumping through my veins. Back and forth he went until I couldn't breathe and on that gasp, Alex slipped between my lips and his tongue laid siege inside my mouth, taming me into submission. I clung to his broad shoulders and pressed my body closer to his, hungry for more even though I shouldn't be.

Alex's hands roamed my body, admiring, no, worshipping my curves. His big hands cradled the small of my back, leaning me over just enough that I was completely at his mercy while he devoured me.

And I let him. Hell, I encouraged it, pressing my

curves against him and holding him tighter. I wanted more. I needed more, and that thought scared the hell out of me.

I pulled back with wide eyes, heart pounding as I realized just how much I wanted this man. "I, um, I need to go do…something." And then like the coward I was, I ran and locked myself in my room.

Chapter 23

Alex

"Go on, taste it." I held a fork of red velvet cake with a tangy buttercream frosting out to Sasha who looked like I was holding nuclear waste for her to taste. "Go on. Don't be shy."

The way she bit down on her bottom lip was enough to make my cock stand at attention. She was hesitant and I couldn't understand why. Just yesterday I'd kissed the hell out of her and she'd clung to me like I was hers, like all of this was real. That was before she ran away like her ass was on fire.

"I can do it myself."

"Of course you can," I replied and rolled my eyes. "But there's a piece right here already. Taste it," I urged and pushed the fork closer until the frosting touched her lips. "Please."

She licked the frosting from her top lip and every inch

of me was hard and aching, ready to relive the last time I'd had her naked and spread out before me. "Fine." Sasha's lips parted into a sinful 'o' and I groaned as I slid the fork between her lips. "Mmm," she moaned, her blue eyes wide with appreciation. "Very good."

I leaned forward with a conspiratorial smile. "Think we can get some of this buttercream to go?" I wiggled my eyebrows until she laughed.

"I'm sure if you use your charm, she'll give you a bucket of it."

I leaned back with a laugh. "A bucket? That's ambitious, but I'm up for the challenge."

"Okay." The pastry chef appeared at the small round table with another set of dessert plates in his hands. "This is German chocolate cake. It's not traditional for a wedding cake, but I was told it was the bride's favorite. I didn't like the way he eyed Sasha with a flirty smile, but I reigned in my temper. All of this effort would be useless if I decked the guy tasked with making our wedding cake.

"Really?" Her blue eyes were wide as she smiled at me. "You told him?" She practically danced in her seat, clapping her hands giddily. "I've never had German chocolate cake made by a professional before."

The chef was so pleased that he served her first, not the famous athlete, but I was fine with it. Sasha had this way about her, of making everyone feel good, from egotistical chefs to even more egotistical hockey players.

"I hope it meets your expectations," he told her and disappeared to give us time to taste and decide.

This time, Sasha didn't have to be asked to taste the cake, she took one bite and then another, and then another, moaning louder with every bite. "Oh. My. God. This is perfect. Absolutely perfect."

I stared at her face, lit up with excitement over cake. I couldn't remember the last woman I was with who even noticed the food beyond its calorie and carb count. "Absolutely perfect?"

She nodded and her face split into a smile. "Oh yeah. Taste it," she said and held her fork out to me.

I didn't wait, I held her wrist and slid the cake from the fork, my gaze never leaving hers. "Holy shit, that *is* good."

"Right?" She looked down at her plate with a frown when she found it empty and slid her arm across the table to steal my plate.

I gripped her wrist and arched a brow. "What do you think you're doing?"

She blinked innocently. "I'm cake tasting. Duh." One finger hooked over the edge of the plate and pulled it closer.

"My cake."

"Our cake," she smiled. "We're engaged, remember?"

"Okay," I agreed. "You can have some."

She relaxed and pulled the plate closer when I grabbed the other edge. Sasha frowned. "You said I could have some."

"I did, but only if you let me feed you." It wasn't right to play with her this way, but it was so fun. Sasha was running from whatever was happening between us and I couldn't blame her. This attraction between us could be fun, or it could make the next two years incredibly complicated.

She rolled her eyes skyward. "The things I do for cake."

"Well now I'm curious, Sash. What things do you do, or would you be willing to do, for cake?"

"Let you feed me," she whispered when I slid the fork between her lips. "For starters." She giggled when I growled in sexual frustration.

"Funny."

She shrugged. "I thought so."

"I'm marrying a comedian," I grumbled and held out another forkful of cake for her. "Lucky me." Sasha leaned forward to take the cake and I switched it out for my lips, kissing her again because I'd waited long enough. It had been too long, more than twelve hours since I had a taste of her and I was starving.

She froze but quickly leaned into me, cupping one side of my face as she deepened the kiss this time. She moaned as she sucked on my tongue, wrapping her fingers through my hair with another moan. She pulled back, face flushed and lips swollen.

"Maybe you're on to something with that buttercream."

I groaned.

Sasha laughed.

We settled on the German chocolate for our wedding

cake, because like every other groom-to-be on the planet, I just wanted to make my woman happy. "I'll go put down the deposit," I told her gruffly, adjusting the evidence of my arousal before the cameras just outside the window caught a glimpse of me with a hard on.

"I recommend the four tier, but we can go bigger if you like," the chef recommended with a smile.

"Let's do five since Sasha loves it so much. And do me a favor, add one two layer cake to be delivered to this address every week until the wedding. Is that something you can handle?"

The chef smiled. "Of course. Who am I to stand in the way of a man and his true love?"

True love? I didn't correct his assumption because what else was he supposed to think? In fact, that was exactly what we were hoping the whole world thought. It was the point of all of this, never mind that hot as fuck kiss I laid or her, or maybe she'd laid it on me. "That's right," I finally settled on before going back to the table for Sasha.

"Everything good with the Chef?"

I nodded. "Perfect. Ready to go?" I held a hand out and she slipped her smaller hand in mine with a grin.

"You know, Alex, we could get two smaller cakes so there's something you like too. This is your wedding as well."

When had a woman ever put my needs and wants first outside of the bedroom? Sasha really was something else. "And miss out on the sounds you make when you eat that cake? Not a chance." She blushed prettily and bumped her shoulder against mine, or tried to with our massive height difference.

"So you want me moaning all during our wedding night, huh?"

"Fuck yeah," I sighed and guided her inside the back of the waiting car. "More than anything, Sash."

She sucked in a sharp breath, eyes wide and nostrils flared at my words. "Alex," she began, but the sound of my phone ringing stopped whatever she was about to say.

"Yeah?"

The voice on the other end of the call belonged to man. It was deep and gruff, and unfamiliar to me. "Alex Witter?"

I frowned. "Who's asking?"

"I'm Raul, the investigator Jack hired. I have news and he said you should be the first to hear it."

I laughed. "Now I know you're full of shit. Jack would never let anyone know something he didn't already know."

The man tried for a laugh but it was forced. "He said you would say that, and he also said, you're a big boy pretty boy, you decide what to do with the info."

Okay that sounded like Jack. "I'm listening."

There was a long silence before the man spoke again.

"Who is it?" Sasha mouthed the words, her gaze focused on my face.

"I found Miriam Juliet Winters."

"You did." It was like a weight had just lifted from my shoulders. "Where is she? Do you have her contact information?"

"Yes and no," Raul hedged. "I found her at Sandstone Memorial Cemetery, her new home as of three weeks ago."

Shit. "Do you have anything else on her?"

"Yes. I'll be in Houston the day after tomorrow and I'll deliver the file I've put together on her."

"Thank you, Raul. I appreciate it."

"Of course. My condolences." He ended the call before I could say anything, which I was grateful for, because what the hell would I say?

"Are you okay, Alex?"

I shook my head. "That was the investigator. Dixie's mom died three weeks ago."

"Oh no!" She slid closer and wrapped me in a tight hug. "I'm so sorry, Alex. This is horrible."

"No," I growled. "What's horrible is that I still don't remember her. The name doesn't ring any bells, and if I close my eyes, I can't see her face. How fucked up is that?"

She shrugged. "What does it matter? Do you remember every woman you've slept with?" Her dark brows arched playfully at the question.

"No," I sighed and shook my head. "But this is different."

"Why, because she got pregnant?"

I nodded and tried to put some distance between us but the stubborn woman would allow it. "Yeah. Obviously."

"Bullshit," she said and gripped my chin, forcing our gazes to lock. "This woman was Dixie's mother and it's okay if that's all she ever means to you. She left you with a wonderful gift and you can love her for that or just be grateful."

"Miriam Juliet, that's her name," I said like that mattered at this point.

"Okay, well learn what you can about Miriam Juliet so that you can tell Dixie what there is to know about her."

I laughed bitterly. "What if she asks if I loved her mother?"

"Then you tell her the truth, that you'll always love her for bringing Dixie into your life but that her dear old dad was a big slut and didn't do love."

I frowned and Sasha laughed. "Great parenting talk, Sash."

She shrugged. "You know, or something like that." She laid her head on my shoulder. "I really am sorry, Alex. I know you were hoping to find her alive." Her hand slid up and down my thigh, the move meant to be comforting rather than arousing.

"So much for answers."

"Maybe not. See if she has any family or left behind any keepsakes that you can save for Dixie when she's older."

I nodded absently. It was a good idea and I would text Raul later, for now I just wanted to bask in her easy affection. "Thank you, Sasha."

She pulled back and looked up in confusion. "For what?"

"For being you. For just being here. Thank you."

"Of course. No matter what else is going on, Alex. We're a team."

"A pretty good one," I agreed and wrapped an arm around her, unable to resist pressing my lips to that sexy smile of hers.

Chapter 24

Sasha

Alex's mouth ravished mine for an eternity. Starting in the car, we barely came up for breath inside the elevator, down the hall and into the penthouse. His mouth had a way of making me lose all sense of space and time, and every pass of his tongue disintegrated a few more of my brain cells. Never mind the way his hands roamed and explored my curves, leaving a white-hot trail of fire everywhere he touched.

"Sasha," he moaned against my lips and pulled me closer. "You're so fucking perfect."

"I'm not," I insisted as we stumbled down the hall and into his enormous bedroom.

"I think you are," he growled and pushed me down on the bed, his big hands made quick work of my jeans and my blouse, leaving me in nothing but pale yellow lace. "So fucking perfect."

When he growled at me like that, an intense look on his face, I wanted to believe that someone found me perfect and beautiful. That he found me more than enough. "Alex," I moaned and pulled him closer.

This time things weren't as frantic. Alex took his time as he peeled off my bra and then my panties, so slowly I shook with my need for him. And when the tables were turned, he vibrated as I undressed him piece by piece until every inch of his gorgeous well-muscled body was bared to me. "Sasha, babe. You're killing me."

I laughed. "Sorry, the view is just so stunning."

His nostrils flared and he backed me up until I fell backwards, his big body, his comforting weight on top of me. "I got the best view in the house." He flashed that too charming, sexy, lopsided grin just before he kissed me. Devoured me. Turned me inside out.

We both took our time, savoring one another as if this was our last night on earth together. He kissed me like I mattered, he kissed me like I was everything he ever wanted or needed in this world. It was a heady experience, the Alex made love to me, the way he touched me and the way he kissed me.

As his body slide into mine everything just felt right. It felt perfect. His soft grunts that grew more intense as his own pleasure grew combined with my cries of pleasure, pleas for more. "Yes, Alex." The words were whispered in his ear and his muscles tensed all around me. "More," I begged and locked my legs around his back.

"So wet," he whispered. "So hot. So fucking good." The last part came out on a growl that I felt all the way down to the center of my heart. He lifted one leg higher and buried his face in the side of my neck, kissing and nibbling my neck and shoulder as he pumped in long, deep strokes that pushed me closer and closer to the edge. "Sasha."

My whispered name unlocked something inside of me and I knew I was in trouble, real trouble because right now what I felt for Alex felt like a lot more than a crush. It felt real and that was a problem. It wasn't.

His hips sped up, pumping slightly faster but deeper and harder, pushing me, urging me to reach for that pleasure just out of reach. "Sasha, babe."

He kissed me again, his tongue thrust in and out in time with his cock and I was lost, I was gone and this man was the cause. Alex kissed me with as much intensity as he pounded into me and nothing, not my thoughts or doubts, could stop the pleasure as it rose to the surface and exploded out of me. "Alex!" I arched into him and my toes curled as I was hit with a wave of pleasure so great and so profoundly intense that it shook my body uncontrollably for several long minutes. "Yes, Alex!"

His hips sped up, moving fast and deep, his mouth dotting kisses on my lips and my neck, down to my collarbone. His green eyes were so intense as they stared down at me that another burst of pleasure shot out of me, triggering his own orgasm. "Fuck, Sasha!" He pumped and pumped even as his jaw clenched and his face twisted in agony. He was beautiful as his pleasure roared out of him and flowed into me, and as he slowed and the delicious weight of him sank into me, I rubbed his back knowing without any doubt in my heart that I was falling for the winger.

Instead of dwelling on that, I enjoyed the heat of his flesh against mine, the feel of his arms wrapped around me as we both drifted off to sleep.

I woke with a start the next morning as the sun filtered through the large windows, looking around to find Alex gone. *Great.* I gathered my clothes, dressed quickly and went to my room to change before checking on Dixie. She wasn't in her room and the sight that faced me in the kitchen was too much for my full heart to bear.

Alex was shirtless—again—with Dixie in his arms as he spoon fed her mashed sweet potatoes and chickpeas. "Morning sleeping beauty."

I felt the blush heat my skin even as I tried to look unaffected. "Morning."

"Sleep okay?" He pulled his lips in tight as if he was trying not to smile.

"Fantastic." I narrowed my gaze at him. "You?"

"Best sleep I've had in ages." He finished feeding Dixie and put her in the highchair, his gaze settled on me. "Bad news. I can't do menu planning today. There's a team charity thing I forgot about."

My immediate reaction was disappointment but I

reminded myself that I had no real claim on Alex or his time. It was just the bucket of ice water I needed on my overheated thoughts and I simply nodded, flashing an understanding smile befitting any wife of convenience. "Sure. No problem."

"I can't get out of it," he explained further, guilt softening his tone.

"It's all right, Alex. Work is your priority. I get it." And maybe this break was just what I needed to get a hold of my emotions before our wedding day. "I'll handle it."

"Thank you." Relief relaxed his broad shoulders and he stood, ready to leave but not before he pressed the sweetest kiss to Dixie's forehead and stopped to give me one too. "See you girls later."

"That was interesting," Henrietta said, a knowing smile on her face.

I didn't bother denying anything. The penthouse was big but it wasn't so big that she hadn't noticed where I'd slept, or where I hadn't. "Thank you for watching Dixie." The venue, the cake and even the invitations were taken care of. Now there was just the menu and we would be good to go.

Before getting dressed for the appointment, I called one of my fellow nannies from the agency to see if she was free. "Hey Toni, it's Sasha."

"What's up, girl? Have you found a new placement yet?"

"Yeah, I'm here now, but that's not what I'm calling

about." I inhaled and on the exhale explained about the wedding and my need for a meal tasting partner.

"Wow," she laughed. "I have so many questions, but not enough time to ask, get the answers or go taste testing with you. Sorry. Try Lucy."

Bummer. "Maybe I will, thanks."

"Yep, and don't think we won't be having a conversation about this soon." With another laugh Toni ended the call.

Lucy and I weren't all that close, but I knew her well enough to ask, but her easy acceptance surprised me. "I'll meet you at the caterer," she said quickly.

An hour later Lucy and I sat at a small table with Dixie and Lena at our sides. "Don't tell anyone but this was my favorite part of wedding planning. For some women it's the dress but for me it was the food." She laughed and her eyes sparkled with pure bliss.

"The cake tasting has been my favorite so far," I admitted. My mind tried to pull up the memories of Alex replacing the cake with his delectable mouth but I shoved them away. "This part isn't bad either." The food was good but making a decision had struck me with fear so palpable that I couldn't move. "I can't choose."

Lucy nodded knowingly. "That's all right. Pick your top two or three from each course and ask if you can take them home to your groom, name dropping him if you have to, so that you can decide together. It'll work, trust me."

"Yeah, okay. Thanks." What in the hell was wrong with me? I'd stood at my mother's side for dozens if not hundreds of events like this and I could normally make these choices in my sleep. This inability to make a decision was definitely about my feelings for my future husband and that just made me mad. "I'll go ask for some to go containers."

Lucy was right, the chef had no problem packing up a few items for me once she realized I was the "regular woman" who got to marry Alex Witter. "I'll bring it to your table."

"Okay, thank you." That was easy enough and I was grateful that Lucy was available today or we might have ended up with hoagie sandwiches for our wedding meal. "She's going to bring out the to-go containers but we're done so you can get back to your day. I appreciate you making time in your day for me, though."

"Are you kidding? We're practically going to be sisters. Dante is a bit of a grump and Alex is his best friend so we'll be seeing a lot of each other over the years."

I looked away because I didn't like to lie but the truth was we would only see each other for the next couple of years and then I would just be the girl that was Alex's first wife.

"Is something wrong?"

"No," I said too quickly. "Nothing at all. Why?"

"No reason," Lucy said just as quickly. "Let's get out of here."

I frowned. "Where are we going?"

Lucy sent me a coy smile. "You'll see."

A thread of worry tightened inside of me but I didn't

think she had any nefarious plans so I strapped Dixie in and followed Lucy in her navy blue Mercedes. We stopped at a gargantuan light brick building without a sign, at least anywhere that I could see. "What is this place," I asked as she and Lena stopped beside the car.

Lucy bounced on her toes. "We're going wedding dress shopping!" She jumped up and down as much as her pregnant body would allow, and then she stopped. "I mean, I assumed you didn't have one yet since you didn't say anything, or show me any photos."

Shit. "I totally forgot." How on earth was I going to sell this story about my relationship with Alex when I totally spaced on what most women consider the centerpiece of their wedding day? The gown. "How could I have forgotten?"

"Pregnancy brain?" Lucy offered with a teasing grin.

"Definitely not."

She frowned.

"I mean, we're careful. Now isn't the right time, with Dixie's arrival and the season starting and all that." Dammit, I was blowing this. "I'm not pregnant. Just forgetful, apparently."

"No worries. We're here and we'll find you something that'll make Alex swallow his tongue."

The thought of Alex seeing me as a woman suitable for him in every way, of him gasping in shock when he caught sight of me in my wedding dress was appealing. But it couldn't happen.

Could it?

"Sasha?" Lucy's concerned expression made me realize I'd spaced out, lost in my own thoughts.

"Oh, sorry. I guess I was just imagining his face when he sees me," I lied. He did say I was perfect and beautiful, though it was in the heat of passion so did that really count? I didn't know but staring at Lucy's hopeful expression made me want to find out.

Chapter 25

Alex

"What do you think?" I stood on the elevated platform in a black tuxedo, arms spread wide and a smile on my face as I looked at Dante through the half-circle of mirrors that surrounded us.

Dante looked me up and down, his gaze assessing like the fashion mogul he was. "Looks good. But are you sure black on black is appropriate for a wedding?"

I frowned. "Why not?"

"You look like a spy or a gangster, especially with your light coloring."

My shoulders slumped. "So I have to go with a basic black and white tux?"

Dante's lips curled into an amused grin. "No. There's a world between a basic tux and this," he waved his hand at the tux. "What does Sasha say?"

His question hit harder than it should. "Nothing. She

hasn't said much about the wedding. Isn't that odd?" The wedding planning was complete except for wedding attire which was why I was putting myself through the hassle of shopping.

Dante shrugged. "Why? The wedding is real but this isn't a love match. Is it?"

It didn't start out that way but I couldn't deny that I felt something for the curvy nanny. "It wasn't supposed to be."

Dante arched a brow. "But it is now?"

I nodded and told him about the news I received about Dixie's mother. "Sasha and I were together when I got the news and you know what she did? Slid closer and soothed me, tried to make me feel better that I didn't remember anything about the woman who had my daughter." I still couldn't believe how kind and caring she'd been at the moment I was sure I deserved it least. "What am I supposed to do about that?"

Dante's lips tugged up into a smile. "Keep her?"

I nodded because that was exactly what I wanted. I could picture it as clear as day since it was the life I lived now, except we snuck around to be together as though we shouldn't be, despite the fact that soon we would be married. "I think I'm falling for her, Dante."

"That's good. Isn't it?"

"It is," I answered easily. "Or it would be if I had any fucking clue how she felt about me." Sasha was a nanny sure, but she came from money which meant she didn't need mine which was a plus. But it also meant she might be worried that I would tarnish her image or lineage or something, especially the whole situation with Dixie.

Dante replaced me on the elevated platform, closely assessing his reflection from all sides. "You know, we could have done this at my place," he grumbled.

"Yeah," I smiled. "But then I wouldn't get to see you being such a grumpy asshole."

He flipped me off and I laughed. How the hell we'd become friends was a perfect storm of events that culminated in both of us dodging fortune hunters at some rubber chicken charity event years ago and from there a friendship was born. A friendship that had seen a lot of ups and downs, which meant I knew my friend was gearing up to tell me something I didn't want to hear. "Have you tried actually talking to Sasha about what or who she wants?"

I snorted and shook my head. "Of course you go straight to talking about feelings. Lucy has trained you well."

"Maybe. Or maybe I just realized that however uncomfortable it is to talk about shit, it's not nearly as uncomfortable as trying to fix something due to a miscommunication."

My gaze narrowed at Dante as I shrugged out of the black tuxedo jacket. "What are you saying?"

"Talking about how you feel now is better than living in limbo."

Yeah, I understood what he was saying but talking about my feelings just wasn't my style. "The thing is, I think she does feel the same. She hasn't said so but when we're naked it feels so perfect, ya know? But afterwards she's skittish and distant."

Dante gave me a look that said he thought I was a dumbass. "So you're having sex but you're not talking about what your relationship will be once you're married?"

My brows knitted into a frown and I nodded because that was exactly it, but Dante's tone, once again, said he thought I was an idiot. "What's there to talk about? We'll be married and having sex, just how it should be. Now neither of us has to go in search of it outside the relationship." It would make everything easier for both of us, and it would appease my sponsorship deals.

Dante shook his head but a ghost of a smile broke through his scowl. "You really are just a pretty face, aren't you?"

I shrugged off his backhanded compliment. "But at least I'm pretty."

"Look Alex, I know the last thing you want to do is open yourself up and be vulnerable with a woman, especially one you haven't known long, but dammit you need to sit down and talk about this. Lay out your expectations before you take the vows."

"Why," I asked seriously. "We're going through with the wedding no matter what."

He let out a frustrated sigh. "Because this whole thing could blow up in your face."

"There are contracts," I insisted weakly. As much as I hated to admit it, Dante was starting to make sense.

"Yes, but you know the number one reason contracts are broken? Because someone's feelings gets hurt. They feel lied to or disrespected or some other emotion that they can't or won't get over. I'd hate to see that happen to you, Alex."

A broken contract. It wasn't something I wanted, not professionally or personally. "You think that could happen?"

He nodded. "I do. What if she doesn't want to continue sleeping together after the wedding for fear she might fall in love with a man who hasn't given any indication that he feels the same?"

"Shit."

"Now he's getting it," Dante said with a small laugh.

"You know, maybe we should have just done this at your place since you're kind of raining on my parade." It was an immature thing to say when he was just trying to help but I was only half kidding.

Dante roared out a laugh and clapped me on the back. "Sorry about that but I'm not sorry. It's time for you to be a grownup about this, man. You don't want to lose Sasha, especially now that you know Dixie isn't going anywhere."

My scowl darkened and my so-called friend laughed louder.

"Just tell her how you feel and give her the choice going into this marriage. Don't just hope it all works out, make it happen."

"How do I do that?"

"The same way you became the best in hockey. Hard work. Effort. Blood and sweat. Tears if it comes down to it."

Dante was right. This was too important, Sasha was too important to leave anything to chance. I was a master at setting a goal and achieving it, like Dante said it was how I became who I was. I just had to do the same with Sasha. "Thanks, man. You've helped a lot."

"Good. Try not to screw it up, Lucy likes Sasha and she thinks she's good for you."

I smiled. "She's right. Lucy is a smart cookie." Sasha was good for me, the only question left was did Sasha think I was good for her.

Only one way to find out.

Chapter 26

Sasha

"Tip's already taken care of, ma'am." The fresh faced delivery guy flashed a smile while I signed the electronic keyboard, took it back and handed me a lavender and yellow box. "Enjoy." He was gone, whistling as he made his way back to the elevator.

I frowned at the box. It was different than the other packages that had been arriving all week from the companies Alex had endorsement deals with, which were often baskets filled with expensive gourmet foods and alcohol, high end wedding gifts even though we didn't have a registry and a few even sent swag. It was odd and unlike anything I've ever experienced before and I had to keep reminding myself that this was all just a fantasy. It was a real fantasy that I would be living for the next couple of years but none of it was real.

None of it, except my feelings for the man who would

be my husband in less than a week. Luckily for me, Alex seemed completely clueless about my feelings, which suited me just fine. He had plenty of time to admit his feelings and since he hadn't, I knew for sure that this was just another part of the convenience factor.

Oh sure, he liked me well enough. He was attracted to me. But Alex didn't want to keep me around beyond the point I was useful.

"What's in the box?" Henrietta's question and her smiling face pulled me from my thoughts and I realized I was just standing in the middle of the living room holding the box while I got lost in my thoughts. Again.

"I don't know. Let's see." I followed Henrietta back to the kitchen, casting a quick look at Dixie's sleeping form on the way. I lifted the lid and gasped at the sight of a smaller version of our wedding cake. "German chocolate cake." Tears sprang to my eyes and I felt foolish. A cake had come last week as well. It was waiting for me when I returned to the penthouse after shopping for a wedding dress.

"Another one? Alex is wooing you," Henrietta said with a sweet smile.

I shook my head, automatically rejecting her words because if I allowed them to seep into my mind and my heart, for even a second, they would take hold and I might start to believe it. "He's just being thoughtful."

"Sasha," she sighed. "Men like Alex don't have to be thoughtful and no offense because I love the boy like he's my own, but he's not exactly known for being thoughtful.

This means something," she insisted. "You mean something to him."

That much was true. The question was, what did I mean to him? Was it just affection or something more? "I'm taking care of his daughter."

Henrietta frowned at me. "You're determined to be obtuse about this, aren't you?"

"No, not determined. I'm just protecting myself." Alex hadn't given any indication that his feelings have changed so I won't assume they have.

Sympathy flashed in her dark eyes and she nodded as if she understood. "All right, if you insist. That cake smells incredible."

I laughed, grateful for her change of topic. "Let's not wait another moment to dig in, then."

Alex found us enjoying large slices of cake and coffee when he returned from practice with damp hair that hung adorably over his eyes. "Cake?"

"Yes," I smiled at him. "Thank you for another cake," I laughed. "But I'm not sure if my clothes will thank you."

Heat flared in his green gaze and they raked over my body as heavy as a caress. "You look good to me," he growled. "And we can always buy new clothes."

"That won't be necessary," I said with a smile as I cut another slice and plated it up, sitting it beside me. "Because there's enough to go around." And because I ate half of the last cake on my own.

Amusement flashed in his eyes as he took the seat

beside me. "Thank you." He leaned forward and smacked a kiss against my cheek.

I inhaled his fresh, masculine scent deeply. He smelled clean and manly, and familiar. The truth was, Alex smelled like home and when he gave out such easy affection it was enough to fool my heart into believing that it was all real. "You're welcome," I answered in a breathy voice.

"Well, I got laundry to do," Henrietta said with a glint in her eyes. "I'll let you lovebirds enjoy your cake in peace." She shuffled off and every part of me wanted to call her back, to tell her we weren't love birds and didn't need any time alone, but she was fast.

"There's something I want to talk to you about." Alex's deep voice broke through and slowly I turned to face him. My heart raced at the serious expression on his face.

"Um okay. What's up?" I hoped that sounded as easygoing as I wanted it to because inside my heart raged and anxiety caused my stomach to do an Olympic level gymnastics floor routine.

"We're getting married soon."

I nodded. "We are. Aren't we?"

His full lips tugged into a smile. "That is still the plan, yes."

I tried to read his body language or the expression on his face to figure out where he was going with all of this, but he gave away nothing. I'll bet he was an excellent poker player. "We're getting married soon, and?"

"And," he sighed, tugging a lock of my hair before he

curled it around his finger. "I think we should talk about our, ah, expectations."

I froze. He seemed so nervous. Too nervous when the contract was signed as this was already a done deal. "I don't expect you to buy me clothes and cars or anything like that." Did he think I would take advantage of his money while we were married? My heart squeezed in pain at the thought that he really didn't know me at all.

His blond brows knitted into an angry vee. "You should expect it since we'll be married and I can afford it. Besides there will be charity events and awards ceremonies that you will be expected to attend with me." He shook his head. "But that's not what I was getting at."

"Okay." I drew the word out to at least three syllables as my heart rate increased. "What are you getting at?"

"I like you Sasha."

I smiled, determined to ignore the blush that rose up my body at his words or the way my heart pounded like a drum against my chest. "I like you too, Alex."

"Good, because I think we should consider-." Whatever else he'd been about to say was cut off by the sound of his phone ringing in his pocket. "Dammit."

Disappointed, I pulled back and flashed a smile I didn't feel. "You should probably get that."

"Yeah," he sighed. "It's Jack."

I didn't know whether to be grateful to Jack or wish horrible things on him, but in the end I just shrugged off the seriousness of the moment and finished my cake before I went back to Dixie.

She was the real reason—the only reason—I was here anyway.

Still my thoughts returned to Alex and to what he'd been about to say. Was he going to say he wanted the marriage to be real? That we should stop sleeping together after the marriage just in case I get the wrong idea? I didn't know, couldn't know and Alex's phone call had lasted more than an hour.

We never did get to finish or even really start that conversation, which I guessed was an answer of sorts all on its own.

A knock sounded on my door and I glanced at the clock. Eleven-fifteen. That meant there was only one person it could be so instead of scrambling to cover myself up, I answered the door in my towel.

"Alex," I sighed as I bit back a smile at his teasing expression. "What's up?"

"I brought you something," he answered and stepped inside—without an invite—with his hands behind his back.

My gaze raked over his bare chest, the low-slung pajama pants that showed off his beautiful body and the bulge beneath. "You're the present?"

His face split into a grin. "Always," he joked. "But no. This is for you." He produced a small tub with a plastic lid on top and handed it to me.

"What is it," I asked as I flipped the top and inhaled

the rich, slightly tangy scent. "Buttercream." My brows dipped in confusion. "You brought me buttercream."

Alex nodded, *oh so* proud of himself. "I brought you buttercream. More accurately," he began and reached between us to tug on my towel until it fell to the ground, "I brought *us* buttercream."

"I'm surprised you didn't bring the left over German chocolate from earlier today." I laughed at the small frown on his face.

"Too messy," he replied with a smile. "And this is going to taste damn good right now."

Before I could ask what he meant, Alex dipped his finger into the tub and scooped out some of the to die for frosting and smeared it down the length of my neck. "Alex," I moaned when his tongue touched my cool skin, sucking and licking the cream until my body was on fire. "Alex," I moaned again.

He pulled back with a heavy-lidded smile. "It's for both of us," he growled, the sound stiffened my nipples to hard, aching peaks. "Me and you," he whispered and swiped frosting across my bottom lip before he kissed it off.

My hand went to his strong arm and I clung to him as he kissed me senseless. I ignored the warning signs that said no matter how good this felt, how irresistible and how magnetic the pull, this was a bad idea. I ignored them and focused on the way he kissed me, like I was his everything.

Alex pulled back, still smiling and it stole my breath. "I like the taste of you better."

My heart hammered in chest at his words which I wanted to believe were genuine and not guided by lust.

"Yeah?" I asked playfully and dipped two fingers inside the tub and wiped it down his chest. "Let's see." I leaned forward and slid my tongue on one side of the frosting and then other before finally the tangy, sweet cream touched my tongue and I moaned.

"Sasha," he growled and fisted one hand in my hair.

"Alex." His name left my lips on a soft moan as I wiped more of the frosting on his nipples.

"Fuck, babe. This wasn't the game I imagined when I knocked."

I laughed and took a step back, tucking my fingers into the waistband of his pajamas and tugged them down. "You said it was for us didn't you?"

He nodded with his jaws clenched tight, his gaze riveted on my movements as I smeared one line of frosting down the hard length of him and dropped to my knees. "Sasha."

I smiled and flicked my tongue along the slit, teasing him by licking off the cream and leaving him unsatisfied. "Needs a little more," I whisper and add more frosting before wrapping my lips around him and sucking the frosting off slowly.

"Ah, fuck, Sash." His hips pushed forward and I took every inch of him, sucking off the frosting until all that was left was Alex. Long and thick, and now slightly sweet on my tongue.

The growls and grunts he let out hit me straight

between the thighs and I grew wetter and hotter, my entire body pulsed with pleasure from giving him pleasure. I sucked him deeper and harder, hollowed my cheeks and swirled my tongue.

"Sasha," he growled and gripped my hair so tight it stung in the best possible way. "Your mouth is perfect. Completely fucking perfect."

I smiled up at him and gripped him tight before I took him to the back of my throat.

"Sasha, oh fuck." His grip tightened on my hair and he pulled me back and stared down at me. "Later I'm going to fuck that sweet mouth of yours but right now I'm dying to be inside you."

"We can't having you dying, now can we?"

"Minx," he grumbled and picked me up, tossing me on the bed before he joined me. "I would lick buttercream from your hot, wet pussy but I think you're sweet enough." Then Alex proved his words true and devoured me, using his lips and tongue—even his teeth—to give me two powerful back to back orgasms that rocked my world. "Mmm, perfectly sweet. Juicy as fuck. Hungry for more."

His words sent shivers down my spine. My fingers tangled in his hair and my hips pushed up to get closer to his delicious mouth. "Alex, what are you doing to me."

"Making you purr," he growled, kissing the inside of my thighs, my hip bones and up to my ribs. He licked the underside of my breasts before he wrapped his lips around my nipples and sucked, nibbled, bit down until I cried out.

"Alex!"

"Yeah, just like that." He gave the other breast the same treatment, sucking and licking until I cried out.

"Yes, Alex. Please."

He released my nipple and kissed his way up my body until we were face to face, mouth to mouth. "I love it when you beg." He took my mouth and slid into my body, in one long, deep stroke. "Fuck, you feel so good."

"So do you." I wrapped my legs around him and locked them, taking him as deeply as I could. "Really fucking good."

He smiled as he pulled back and thrust again, deeper and slower but so much more intense that I felt every inch of him. Every stroke filled me up, stretched me out and pushed me closer to the edge. He was everywhere, all around me, deep inside of me, covering me. "Sasha."

No other words were needed after that, just our names. His name fell from my lips and mine from his as our bodies came together in a beautiful dance that seemed to go on forever. His hips pumped and thrust into me over and over, so deep and so intense that goosebumps covered my flesh.

I arched into him, gripped him tighter and closer. My nails scraped down his back and my eyelids fluttered shut. Something about this felt different. It felt bigger, more important than the other times we've been together. I couldn't put my finger on it except to say that my heart was involved.

"Sasha." I wasn't sure if he said my name or if I imagined it, but something about it triggered my release.

It was powerfully explosive and my body shook uncontrollably as it hit me in wave after wave of pleasure. Tears pricked my eyes and I let them fall as I fell into the dark waves and let them fling me about while Alex plunged deeper and deeper in search of his pleasure. "Yes!"

His grunts grew louder and his thrusts were deeper and harder.

"Fuck me, Alex. Just. Like. That." The words flew from my mouth in breathless grunts.

Alex nibbled my ear and then moved to the curve of my neck where he sank his teeth into my flesh and pounded harder into me.

"Yes, Alex!" My words had an effect on him, pushed him deeper. His thrusts were more intense and I took every inch of him, pulsing and squeezing all around him. "I'm going to come again."

He hitched my legs up over his hips and pounded so hard the sounds of our hips smacking together echoed in the air, punctuating the intensity of our coming together. His grunts came faster and then he took my mouth in a fiery kiss that prolonged my orgasm until another exploded out of me.

"Alex!" He swallowed the shout and kissed me so deeply that I felt my heart hand itself over to him. It was dangerous, I knew that, but I didn't care, not when I felt so good. Not when *he* made me feel so good. So wanted.

So loved.

It wasn't real and it couldn't last, but I let myself bask

in the moment, in the afterglow while Alex filled me with his pleasure before he collapsed on top of me. I held him close while his breathing returned to normal. When it was all over, I turned away and listened for the sound of his quiet exit.

Only it never came, he wrapped his arms around me and held me close as I drifted off to sleep. I guess this means that my earlier worries about Alex wanting to halt the intimate aspect of our fake relationship was unfounded.

Chapter 27

Alex

"Gotta get home to the old ball and chain?" Greg was the other starting winger on the Highlanders and my closest friend on the team. He loved to give me shit any day of the week, more so now that I was engaged and would very soon be married. "And so it begins."

I looked around the table at my other teammates. These were the men who'd made up my social circle for years, they were young, and most of all, they were single. Soon I wouldn't be either of those things. I laughed off Greg's words and shrugged.

"If you had a woman at home as beautiful as mine, you wouldn't want to spend time with these ugly schmucks either."

"She's smokin' hot," one of the rookies added a little on the loud side. "All those curves too? Witter's a very lucky man."

I narrowed my gaze at the rookie. "Thanks. But watch it."

"Whoa," Greg joked and held up both of his hands defensively. "The papers and the photos are right, you're totally in love with this chick."

"Duh, we're getting married."

Greg nodded. "When do we get to meet her?"

"At the wedding. I don't want you all scaring her off before it's official."

The truth was my own behavior, or rather my cowardice, was the thing that might have scared her off. I'd come back from practice with the intention of laying all my cards on the table and telling her how I felt, but I was interrupted by Jack. Okay, I let Jack interrupt us. It turns out that the suits at St. Bay Lager were ready to sign a very lucrative endorsement deal and I'd rushed off to sign it. It was business, I told myself because that was easier than the prospect of telling Sasha my feelings and having her reject me.

Later that night, I thought I would try and talk to her again. I took the buttercream to her room as a joke, I way to ease my way into the conversation I awkwardly ran from before. But, as usual with Sasha, one thing let to another, and before I knew it, we were fucking. And hell if I was going to stop that to talk.

"More puck bunnies for me," Greg interrupted my thoughts with a satisfied smile. "Send the missus my love."

"Yeah, I won't be doing that. See you in the morning," I said to the table at large before I turned to leave the bar. I wasn't in the mood to drink and yuck it up with the team, but I hadn't been out with them all season and that kind of bonding was important. I couldn't let it slide even though I missed Dixie and Sasha, and I couldn't wait to get home to see them.

The penthouse was quiet and mostly dark except for one light that Sasha kept on, joking that we couldn't risk me hurting my money makers in a freak accident with a coffee table. My shoulders slumped in disappointment when I realized it was late, too late to spend any time with Dixie. That didn't stop me from peeking in for a quick look at her sweet sleeping form. Her red hair, growing thicker by the day, stood up all around her head like a halo.

"Sleep well, baby girl."

I hesitated outside of Sasha's room. I wanted to knock and go inside, to tell her how I felt and taste her sweet lips, yet I stood on the other side of the door and contemplated.

For five fucking minutes.

The door swung open and Sasha ran right into me. Instinctively my arms flew out to catch her and hold her close.

"Alex. What are you doing?" She stepped back and looked up at me, sexy and rumpled in her tiny cotton pajamas. "Alex?"

I smiled. "I was debating on whether or not to bother you."

"It's no bother, what's up?" She stepped around me and nodded for me to follow her. "Is everything all right?"

"Not really, no." What in the hell was I saying?

She stopped just inside the living room and turned to me with a question in her blue eyes. "Want to talk about it?"

"Yes," I nodded and raked a hand through my hair. "No," I then said with a smile. "It's complicated."

"Well that's about as clear as mud," she laughed that sexy, throaty laugh that invited the listener to join in.

"I missed you," I blurted out and then flashed a nervous smile. My eyes roamed over her beautiful face, free of make up, her lush pink lips drew my gaze first, and then those big blue eyes. But dammit, the sight of her in hot pink shorts and a matching camisole had my cock waking up and taking notice.

Her eyes widened as if my words surprised her. "I've been right here, Alex."

"I know, but I just wanted to tell you."

"Well we'll be married soon and I'm sure you'll be sick of seeing my face day in and day out." Despite her words, heat flared in her gaze and her nipples hardened to stiff peaks before my eyes.

"Doubtful," I growled and took a step closer.

Sasha took a step back. "Alex."

"Sasha," I growled and closed the gap between us, holding her close enough that her quick breaths fanned over my face. "I've missed you. The taste of you and the feel of you under me."

She sucked in a sharp breath and tilted her head back, giving me an excellent view not just of her cleavage but the pulse fluttering in her throat. "Alex."

She licked her lips and the last bit of my control snapped.

My mouth crashed down on hers and instantly all the doubts and anxiety faded until Sasha was the only thing I could see or hear or feel. Her familiar curves under my hands settled my racing mind but ramped up the beat of my heart.

Sasha wrapped her arms around me and held on tight, pulling me closer like she was as desperate and as hungry for me as I was for her. That eagerness sent fire rushing through my veins and intensified my need for her. Her hands spread wide as they slid up and down my back, as if she were trying to touch as much of me as possible. A groan escaped and I swallowed it down, so damn hungry for her that I could hardly think straight.

She moaned again and I knew there wasn't one damn thing in the world I wouldn't do to get inside her, so I dropped down on the sofa with Sasha on top of me, the weight of her, the softness of her hands and her curves more than I could bear without losing control even further.

"Ah," she groaned and sucked in a breath when she ripped her mouth from mine with a wild-eyed smile. "Alex," she moaned and rolled her hips against my cock, straining beneath my zipper. "Fuck."

My hands gripped her tighter as the expletive fell from her mouth and she continued to grind on me, to take her pleasure from me. It wasn't enough, not at the moment. "Sasha," I growled breathlessly. One hand left the curtain of silk that hung around her shoulders and slid down her back and over her hip, finding silky smooth thighs that grew hotter and hotter as I neared her apex. Two fingers slipped underneath the shorts and then the waistband of her panties. "You're so fucking wet already."

She smiled and let her head fall back with a moan, thrusting her hips towards my touch. "That was the point, wasn't it?"

My cock strained again and I attacked her mouth once more, plunging two fingers in long, deep strokes that drew the most delicious sounds from her, which I was happy to swallow. She was so fucking responsive and all I wanted was to replace my fingers with my cock.

She pulled back with a devilish grin. "Alex," she whispered against my lips. "I need you."

Those were the three words I wanted to hear. "Keep your eyes on me," I commanded, still thrusting deep until I felt the telltale clench of her pussy around my fingers. "On me," I grunted as her blue eyes fluttered shut.

Her eyes opened wide and stayed fixed on me as she rode my hand to her first orgasm. Instead of fluttering shut, they went wide as pleasure swamped her and shook her body. "Oh!" A low growl of satisfaction escaped as she continued to study my face. "You're beautiful," she whispered.

"Hey, that's my line, gorgeous." My fingers slipped out of her body and went straight to my mouth. "So fucking sweet," I murmured around my fingers, smiling at the way her eyes rounded in shock and then her cheeks turned a stunning shade of red.

"Alex," she moaned.

"Put me inside of you, Sash."

Skin still flaming red, she pushed back and dropped to her knees, unfastening my belt and jeans before she freed my cock, stroking it in long, slightly rough up and down movements guaranteed to keep my attention. "Somebody is ready to play." Before I could say a word she flicked her tongue over the slit, swiping away the bead of pearly liquid at the tip. "Mmm," she moaned and wrapped her lips around my cock.

"Sash, babe. I'm on edge here."

She smiled up at me, cock still in her mouth and winked. She fucking winked and took me deeper, leaving me powerless to do anything other than watch my cock disappear between those lush pink lips. Over and over she took me deeper and my eyes started to close but I opened them wider, refusing to look away from one erotic moment of her pleasing me with her mouth.

"Sasha," I warned her because I was dangerously close to losing my shit.

Her answer was to take me deeper until I hit the back of her throat.

"Fuck," I grunted and thrust up, going even deeper.

She swallowed, and then smiled.

Stars burst behind my eyes and I knew I wasn't going to last long.

I didn't have to worry, she teased me until beads of

sweat popped up along my hairline and dripped down my spine, and just when I was ready to pop, the minx stood and shimmied out of her pajama bottoms before she straddled me with a smile.

"Next time, I'm finishing in that pretty mouth of yours."

"Promises, promises," she smiled as she gripped my cock in one hand and my hair in the other, blue eyes boring into me as she impaled herself on my erection. "Oh, my fuck!"

Exactly how I felt as I gripped her hips and helped her set a punishing pace. Her legs trembled with the pleasure of my cock filling her up, her skin reddened at the exertion but in all of that, Sasha's gaze never left mine. She was so damn gorgeous she took my breath away as she fucked my cock, using me for her pleasure. Bringing us both to the brink of madness. "Babe," I growled when my balls tightened and electricity buzzed through my spine.

She smiled and put her mouth to mine, taking me in short, shallow thrusts that quickly pushed her right into the middle of orgasm two. Sasha moaned her pleasure against my mouth and my only regret was that I couldn't see her face twisted in orgasmic agony.

But then she slammed down against me, her sweet pussy pulsing rapidly, tearing my orgasm from my body with the force of a hurricane. She tumbled into a third orgasm, body quivering and convulsing all around me, her teeth nibbled my bottom lip as if she needed something, anything to tether her to earth.

"Sweet Jesus, that was incredible," she said when she finally released me. "You should miss me more often."

I couldn't help but smile at her words. Masculine pride swelled inside my chest and I held her tight against me, letting her feel every drop of me invading her body. "I don't have to miss you at all, not anymore."

She laughed. "Oh yeah, why is that?"

I gripped her hips and thrust up one final time before I gripped her chin between my thumb and forefinger, letting her eyes focus on mine so she could see that I was serious when I spoke. "Because you're mine, Sasha. All mine."

Chapter 28

Sasha

Tomorrow I'll be a married woman. That thought pulsed through me all day long, or maybe it was just the man I was marrying who had me feeling as if I was floating. Alex said he missed me and that had to mean something, didn't it? *Yeah, he missed having sex with you.* That's what the cynical part of my brain insisted but my heart said otherwise.

This was turning into something more than convenience. More than a business transaction.

I hope.

Dixie was sound asleep in her crib and I knew she would be for the next few hours, which made it oh so tempting to creep down towards Alex's media room where he was reviewing game footage. I stand in the hall just outside of Dixie's room and weigh my options. Slip off my panties and go tempt him into being bad with me or wait until our wedding night to have him again. I smiled at the thought of surprising him and pushed on my bedroom door to prepare for seduction.

The doorbell rang.

With a groan I retraced my steps back down the hall and to the front door. It had to be Jack this late in the evening, which meant more business talk and my seduction plans were on hold anyway. I found a small smile as I opened the door but it quickly faded at the sight of the unexpected visitors. "Mom. What are you doing here?" And more importantly why hadn't she called first.

My mother stiffened at my question, clutching her Chanel purse tight to her side as if worried someone might steal it. "That's a fine greeting for your mother."

I bit back the smart retort on the tip of my tongue. "Well it's exactly the greeting one should expect when they show up unexpectedly." I stepped back and waved my parents inside the penthouse. I tried to keep the annoyance off my face and out of my expression and ushered them into the living room. "How are you?" I directed the question to my mother, offering little more than a tolerate pseudo smile for my father.

"Good. You look tired," Mom offered in her patented hypercritical way. "You need to rest up for your big day."

"Thanks, Mom," I deadpan. "So glad you showed up just to tell me I look like shit."

"Language," she gasped, hand to her chest as if she was some southern debutante rather than an east coast blue blood.

"We're here for a reason," my father began slowly. "Have you discussed a prenuptial agreement?"

I rolled my eyes. "Stop right there," I told him coldly. "Alex has more money than I do so it's unnecessary." Even with my trust, he's has far more money than me.

"We are just looking out for you," Mom said in an offended tone. "And he does have a reputation with the ladies."

I laughed bitterly. "Is that your threshold for a terrible husband, fidelity? Well Alex loves me and I love him." I sucked in a breath at that unintended admission. Well, half-admission. I loved him but how he felt about me was anybody's guess.

"Don't get emotional," Dad began.

"I am not emotional," I replied coolly. "And don't think that just because you're sober for once that you get to offer any advice on my relationship."

"Sasha!"

"No," I shot at Mom. "Alex and I love each other and he appreciates me just as I am. He loves me and he doesn't try to change me. If that's not enough to ease your mind, that's too damn bad."

"Without a prenup he might have a right to your trust."

I closed my eyes and reached for patience. "For the last time, Alex is the wealthy one in this relationship. He doesn't need my money and I don't need his, end of story." I shook my head. "I guess you didn't come by to see me because you missed me." Of course they hadn't. The only thing my parents truly cared about was keeping up appearances.

"Of course we missed you," Mom said, her tone once again offended. "It's our job to look out for you."

"Yeah, since when?" Where was that concern when my father spent twenty-three hours of every single day drunk, leaving me to handle too much responsibility because she was more concerned about him. "You weren't looking out for me when I had to write the checks to pay the household staff because someone forgot. Or when you let your friends get handsy because you were too drunk to worry about your teenage daughter. Or,"

"Yes, I got it Sasha. I failed you as a parent."

"Exactly that. I invited you to my wedding, not to offer unsolicited advice on my marriage. Maybe that was my mistake."

Mom sucked in a sharp breath. "No. We appreciate the invitation. It was quite unexpected."

"I didn't want you to feel embarrassed by not receiving an invite," I offered as an olive branch. "I know how important appearances are to you." The invitation allowed them to pretend that everything between us was perfect.

My father rose from the sofa first. "I guess we will see you at the wedding, then."

"I'll be there," I assured him, stiffly accepted a hug from both of my parents.

"You'll have to forgive him, forgive us both at some point," she whispered in my ear.

"Hard to forgive when you haven't apologized or

acknowledged you've done anything wrong." I hugged her back quickly and put some distance between us. "I'll see you both tomorrow."

Completely drained after that short interaction, I pressed my back against the door once my parents were gone and let out several shaky breaths as I realized my hands shook fiercely. I knew exactly why.

The admission.

I was in love with Alex Witter, star winger for the Houston Highlanders. I loved the man I was set to marry in a few hours. *And divorce in a couple of years,* my inner pragmatist offered up easily. The moment I said the words to my parents I knew they were true. Saying them felt right. There wasn't a hint of shock or panic at saying the words, or any guilt over lying because it wasn't a lie.

I loved Alex.

Now the question was, do I let him know that my feelings have changed or should I simply keep it to myself? He didn't sign up for love, he signed up for a convenient wife and caretaker for his daughter, nothing more. Adding my feelings to the mix would only complicate the next two years of our life together.

That wasn't the biggest problem, however. How could I love Alex and continue to enjoy the sensual benefits of being married for the next two years without falling deeper in love with him?

The simple answer was, I couldn't.

The reality was, I would leave this marriage with a

broken heart and now that I knew the truth of my own feelings, there was nothing I could do about it.

Chapter 29

Alex

Practice today was brutal. Between two hours of training and another two on the ice, my body ached and the ice bath with the trainer hadn't helped much. The shower however started to ease the ache in my muscles, and with each passing minute the powerful spray worked its magic.

The bathroom door opened and my brows dipped. I was in my personal bathroom in my bedroom, and the only person who ever came in was Henrietta. "In the shower," I called out since she wasn't expecting me to find me in here but there was no response and no sound of the bathroom door closing to give me privacy.

The glass door slid open and before I turned to see her, the floral scent that was Sasha hit my nostrils. "Good," she purred. "This is exactly where I was hoping to find you. How was practice?"

"Not bad." It was almost a question because she

surprised me. A welcome fucking surprise, but a surprise nonetheless. "Oh," I growled when her hands went to my back and her fingertips dug into the shoulders. "Fuck."

"So tight," she moaned. "Rough day?"

I nodded.

Her lips pressed against the center of my back. "Poor, Alex."

"Sasha," I moaned her name and let my head fall forward as she massaged and kissed me.

"I'll help you relax."

"Already. Are." The words came out on a heavy pant I didn't recognize. "Fuck, so good."

Her hands, small and delicate yet so fucking capable of making me feel good as they slid down on either side of my spine and to my ass. "So tight. So hard." Sasha's words were low and filled with heat. "Beautiful."

I turned and backed her against the wall. "Sasha," I growled.

Her reply was to press a kiss to my chest. My ribs. My abs. She repeated the move on the other side of my body and kissed her way down until she reached my hip bones. Down on her knees, she looked up at me with a flirtatious smile. "Yes, Alex?"

My nostrils flared and heat filled my body. She licked her lips and my cock, hard and aching since she put her hands on me, twitched in her direction. "Fuck." I hissed out the word when she flicked her tongue along the slit. "Sasha, babe."

"I'm helping you relax, Alex. Don't you want that?"

"More than any-fucking-thing."

"Good." She flashed another quick smile before she wrapped one hand and then the other around my dick and squeezed as she brought it to her mouth. "Salty. Clean. Masculine." She hummed as she sucked and licked me, taking me deep until I hit the back of her throat. "Mmm," she moaned again.

"Sasha," I growled as my hips moved, suddenly having a mind of their own. She took me deeper and deeper, cupping my sac as she slurped me up, tasting every inch of me like I was the finest delicacy in the world. "Oh, fuck babe." I watched, unable to look away as she took my cock in her mouth and made me feel so fucking good that there was no longer a doubt how I felt about her.

With her eyes closed and a slight smile on her face interrupted only by my cock pushing between her lips, she looked happy. And when those eyes opened up to me, she was turned on. Sucking me off was turning her on and that made my cock impossibly harder.

"Sasha."

Her answer was to grip my ass cheeks and take me deeper and faster, giving me everything she had until I gave in and filled her mouth with my release.

"Oh fuck, Sasha. Babe." One hand shot out to smack against the shower wall to brace myself as my legs wobbled. She sucked even after I was spent, even as my cock grew soft, the sensitive sensation not unwelcome yet overwhelming. "Sasha."

She sucked as she pulled away until only the tip of my cock was between her teeth and her tongue teased my cock head. She moaned and finally released me. "Feel better?"

I shook my head back and forth, gripping her arms to bring her to her feet. "Fuck yes. I feel incredible." And I wasn't done with her, not by a long shot.

"Good. Enjoy the rest of your...oh!"

I pulled her back into the shower, stopping her attempt to leave. "Where do you think you're going?"

She smiled. "To dry off and get back to...things."

"Things?" I arched a brow and waited for a real answer.

Sasha laughed. "Yeah. Things. It's what I do."

The sound of her laughter was perfect as it echoed inside the shower. She was the only woman I could be naked with and still laugh. "Not yet. I have things I want to do," I growled and brought my lips down against her neck and collarbone as my hands slowly danced down her body.

Her breath hitched and one hand slipped into my hair. "Alex," she moaned when my tongue swirled around the hollow in her throat.

I finally made it to the scorching heaven between her thighs where she was hot and wet, damn near pulsing for me. "You're so fucking wet already. You want me, don't you?"

She nodded.

"You want me to fuck you and make you come?"

"Yes, please."

"Such a sweetheart," I growled and dipped two fingers inside her pussy. "You like that don't you?

She shook her head. "I love it. You fill me up so good."

Her words hit my cock and I grew hard again. Her hips pushed back and slid my other hand up and around her wet hair, giving it a sharp tug. "Fuck my hand, Sash. Make yourself come."

Desire darkened her gaze but she didn't hesitate, rolling her hips and gripping my wrist while she rode my fingers. "Alex. So good. So dirty."

"You're fucking beautiful when you take charge," I growled. It was true, she bit down on her bottom lip and rode out her pleasure, her gaze locked on mine. "You're so close, I can feel your pussy fluttering and squeezing my fingers.

"Alex. Please." She moaned and her eyes fluttered but they didn't close as if she couldn't look away. My thumb found her clit and that was all it took for her to explode around me, body shaking as expletives fell from her lush lips. "Oh fuck," she cried out as her orgasm went on and on because I refused to let it die out. It was too perfect, *she* was too perfect for this moment to end. Her nails dug into my skin and she held on as her body convulsed wildly, riding out each new aftershock.

"So fucking gorgeous," I growled at the satisfied smile that spread across her face at my words.

"That was crazy," she said on a laugh.

"The crazy part is," I began and spun her so she faced the wall. "That we're not even done yet," I whispered in her ear.

Sasha shook her head and glanced at me over her shoulder. "No. I want to see you. I love watching you come."

I spun her around so quickly her legs wobbled. "Don't look away," I commanded and lifted her up, pressing my chest against hers so she was sandwiched between me and the shower wall.

"Like I even could," she panted as she reached down and gripped my cock, stroking it hard and fast.

Just the way I liked it. "Good." A low growl escaped when she lined our bodies up and let gravity help her as she sank down on my length. "Fuck, so good."

"I'm watching," she whispered and licked her lips. "Now, fuck me please."

"Such good manners." I smiled and gripped her hair tight, licking her neck while I thrust deep. Hard and deep.

"Yes, just like that, Alex." She smiled through clenched jaws, her eyes were dark and glassy. "More. Give me more."

"Bossy," I grunted with a smile. "I like you bossy," I told her and gave her even more. Harder and deeper and faster. "Fuck you feel so damn good Sasha."

"You do too." She clenched around me so tight my eyes rolled back. "Watch," she teased, smiling when my gaze clashed into hers once more.

"You feel too good," I admitted, groaning when she clenched around me again.

"Alex, you're making me crazy."

"Excellent." I fixed my mouth to hers and kissed her like crazy while I pounded into her, got lost in the feel of her pussy clenched around me. Her nails dug deeper and nothing felt better than making a woman so crazy with need that she left her mark.

Sasha's cries grew louder and wilder. She pumped her hips against me as her breaths came out faster, shallower. She moaned into my mouth and bit my lip. Her passion swelled and she pumped harder. Faster. "Alex," she mumbled into my mouth with a smile.

Tingles began at the base of my spine and crawled up my back, a sure sign my pleasure was imminent. I tore my mouth from hers and our gazes locked once again. "Sasha."

"I feel you growing and getting harder inside of me." She smiled. "I'm ready if you are."

"So fucking ready," I growled, smiling back.

"Then let's go."

I braced my feet wide against the edges of the floor and gripped her hips, lifting and lowering her on my shaft faster and faster. Her cries grew louder and wilder.

"Alex, yes!" Her body went stiff and then jerked wildly as her orgasm erupted and yanked my own free. "Alex!" She whispered my name over and over as her body shook in my arms.

The more her body clenched, the harder I came right

along with her. "Sasha, oh fuck, Sasha!" I don't know how long we stayed in the shower staring at each other in wide-eyed wonder at what we'd just done. At intensity that erupted between us.

Shocked.

Thoroughly wrecked.

Sasha spoke first. "Not to be greedy but I could definitely go for round two."

My heart slammed against my chest as a smile spread from ear to ear. There's something so sexy about a woman wanting a man so viscerally and so honestly. "Nothing wrong with a woman knowing what she wants, especially when what she wants is me."

"She does," she purred. "She really does."

I carried her to my bedroom and gave her—gave us both—what she wanted until we were too tired to do anything about the desire that still lingered between us.

* * *

"Are you sure you're ready for this?" Dante stood in front of me, straightening my bowtie because he was anal retentive about things like this. "Marriage is a big step. Very big."

I nodded quickly even though I wasn't sure at all if I was ready. "Yeah, I think so."

Dante's brows dipped. "Are you at least prepared to treat Sasha the way she deserves?"

I nodded easily. Last night I heard the way she championed me to her parents, the thing she said in my defense. When she told them she loved me, I was more than a little tempted to believe her. No one had ever defended me like that before. There was no need. I was a man who didn't ask much from the women in his life, just a night or two of fun and then nothing else. "Were you, um, worried on your wedding day?"

Dante flashed a wide smile. "Fuck yeah, I was. I felt sure of my feelings for Lucy but I wasn't sure if I could be the man she needed."

Yeah, that was exactly how I felt. "And how did you become sure?"

"I took one look at her and I knew, without a fucking doubt, that I would do whatever was necessary to keep that beautiful smile on her face." His smile told me everything I needed to know. "But I love my wife. For real."

The door flew open and Jack strode in with a big ass, arrogant grin on his face. His thousand dollar tuxedo was so over the top I couldn't help but grin at the spectacle he made. "Good morning, fuckers. Are we ready to get this over and done with?"

I frowned at Jack's words. The way he spoke about the day rubbed me the wrong way but I kept those words to myself. "As soon as Dante gets my tie perfect, we'll be ready."

Jack barked out a laugh. "You sure you're ready to take up the old ball and chain?"

"That's not how I think of Sasha," I assured him.

She wasn't an obligation or a responsibility. Hell, most nights I counted down the time until I could be with her.

Jack laughed again as if it was the funniest joke in the world. He clapped me on the back and shook his head. "Just get through the ceremony and the monkey dance, and we'll find a way for you to get your needs met. That's what I'm here for."

I frowned and when my gaze slid to Dante's, he was frowning too. "That's not necessary," I assured him but my words fell on deaf ears.

"Of course it is," Jack said around a loud guffaw. "I'll make sure it's discreet. Maybe an apartment on the other side of Houston to make sure the *little lady* is kept in the dark." His elbow nudged me in the side as if we were both willing co-conspirators. "You'll get to be Alex Witter, man about town and faithful husband and family man. The best of both worlds."

I should have told Jack to shut the fuck up. I should have been a man and told him that he sounded like an asshole, that I wasn't looking for anyone to satisfy my needs but my soon-to-be wife. But I didn't. Today was my wedding day and even though Sasha and I weren't going into this with blinders on, it felt monumental. It felt momentous, taking vows and promising to be good to each other until the end of time.

It felt like I should mean it even though our relationship came with an expiration date. "Jack," I growled.

His dark eyes widened and he nodded. "Mum's the

word," he said and winked dramatically. "I'll go make sure everything is on track."

"Why don't you just take your seat," I asked. Jack had been drinking, that much was certain, and I couldn't risk him saying anything disrespectful to Sasha. Not today.

Not ever.

"He's an ass," Dante said easily, finally satisfied with the state of my bowtie.

I nodded. "He is that, but he's also damn good at his job. If not for him, I wouldn't be the man I am today."

"Maybe. But his big mouth is guaranteed to cause trouble for you down the road." Dante's brows knitted into concern. "He doesn't need to pat himself on the back quite so hard for doing his fucking job."

"He's proud," I insisted.

"Too proud," Dante added with a dark scowl on his face. "Just be careful that his mouth doesn't ruin something good."

"This isn't like you and Lucy."

Dante grinned. "If you say so, Alex." He smoothed my lapels and took a step back, assessing my appearance until he was pleased. "You look as good as you're going to. Good luck, man."

I accepted his handshake with a grin. "I guess this is really happening."

"It is," Dante grinned. "Too late to back out now."

"No fucking way am I backing out." An image of Sasha flashed in my mind, her sweet smile and sexy mouth, the way she wasn't overly impressed with me and didn't let me use my charm to win her over. "I'm ready."

"Let's get you married, then."

Words I didn't expect to hear for at least another decade, but when Dante spoke them, I didn't feel fear or worry, only excitement.

Only joy.

And anticipation.

Chapter 30

Sasha

"I now pronounce you husband and wife," the officiant said with a proud smile. "You may now kiss your bride."

I hardly remembered the wedding ceremony other than this last moment and the officiant's proud smile, which was probably for the best. *To think, I was falling in love with this selfish jerk and he was planning to rent an apartment to keep up his whorish ways.* Anger rushed through my veins as humiliation burned through my flesh at the way I defended him to my parents last night, the hope I held in my heart—however secretly—that what we had would become more. I tilted my head up with a half-hearted smile to accept Alex's kiss because that was what was expected of me. That was part of the deal and I was a woman of my word.

Alex kissed me like he meant it, like the vows we repeated meant something to him. He cradled my face in his big hands and smiled down at me with something that looked a lot like love in his deep green eyes. A foolish woman, or rather one who hadn't heard the post-nuptial plans, would have swooned at the words.

Instead, I bit the inside of my jaw to stop the tears that threatened to fall. I wanted to cry because the words I said to my parents were true, the feelings I conveyed were genuine. I loved Alex and he did see me. He saw me for who I was and he appreciated that. He didn't want me to change, but he also just didn't want me.

That's fine, I told myself as Alex lowered his mouth to mine. He didn't have to love me, it was his right to fall for whomever captured his heart. I wouldn't punish him for not sharing my feelings because that wouldn't be right. And there was no need to punish him when my feelings would be punishment enough. I accepted Alex's kisses but I didn't return it the way I would have last night. It was a chaste kiss perfect for a wedding, and that was all I had in me to give.

Alex pulled back with a look of confusion on his face, but ever the professional he shrugged it off, clasped our hands together as we walked into the blazing Texas sun.

"We did it," he whopped. "We're married!" Alex's excitement was contagious even though I knew it was an act. He picked me up and spun me around. "Ready to celebrate?"

I wanted to say yes—badly. It was impossible to look into his joyful expression, his inviting smile and shit all over it on today of all days, but I just didn't have it in me to pretend. Not today. Now right now. I extricated myself from Alex's strong hold the moment we were alone and took a few steps back to gain some distance.

"Sasha?"

My smile was sad and heartbroken because that's exactly what I was. "I'm not really in the mood."

Alex frowned, his hands cupping my jaws as his eyes examined me for any sign that all wasn't right with me. "What's wrong?"

"Nothing is wrong," I sighed. "The wedding is over, we are officially married now."

"Exactly why we should be celebrating." His smile never wavered and I realized what a practiced liar my husband was.

"You don't have to pretend anymore, Alex." I motioned around the bridal suite, empty except for us. "I can now go back to my job and you," I patted his chest gently and tried for a grin I didn't feel. "You can head to your secret apartment and celebrate your life going on as usual." I wanted to say more, to tell him that I would have given him everything if only he wanted it, but I couldn't. Another rejection would be too much to handle so I looked away and then I walked away, holding my tears at bay while I stopped to accept well wishes and words of congratulations from our wedding guests.

An hour later I slipped out of the reception venue and into the back of a waiting limousine. I closed the privacy window and let myself cry for the future I wouldn't have, at least not with Alex. I cried until there were no more tears, until the ache in my heart dulled, until it no longer hurt to think about Alex giving his love, his big strong body to someone else.

I cried until I just couldn't cry anymore, vowing that it would be the last time I cried over Alex or any man. I wouldn't waste a drop of tears on my father or the sins of his past, or any other person. Period.

By the time I made it back to the penthouse, my eyes were red but dry, my body felt heavy and sad, but I was ready to move on to what came after the wedding.

I was ready to move on to everything else, whatever that entailed, and I knew I would have to do it alone.

Without Alex.

He was my husband in name only and if I was silly enough to get my heart involved in this marriage of convenience, well that was totally on me. It wasn't his burden to bear. It was mine alone and I would take care of it.

On my own.

Turns out I wasn't enough. Again.

Chapter 31

Alex

Turns out a wedding reception isn't much fun without a bride. I couldn't say how long I stayed at the reception after Sasha left, only that it felt like a fucking eternity had passed without her. I was miserable and worse I was doing a shit job of looking anything but miserable.

"Where's the happy bride?" Dante stood towering over me, his body casted a long shadow that matched my mood perfectly.

"She's gone," I grunted. "Heard Jack's words apparently and convicted me without a trial."

Dante grunted which I suppose meant he was on my side. He grabbed two flutes filled with champagne and sat. "What was she supposed to think? You didn't correct Jack at all."

"I didn't think she was spying on me. How could I?"

What was she even doing outside the groom's suite in the first place?

"Maybe she came to tell you something and what she heard made it unnecessary."

I frowned. "What does that mean?"

"Nothing."

"Bullshit. You can't say some ominous shit like that and not back it up. What does that mean?"

He shrugged. "Lucy said she got the feeling that Sasha's feelings for you were real, but my wife doesn't know everything."

Shit. Those words ricocheted through me with the force of a bullet. Could that really be true, that Sasha's feelings for me had grown during our time together? Had she come to tell me she wanted our marriage to be real in all ways? "Fuck."

"I'm guessing that's news to you?"

I nodded. "She didn't say anything."

"Why would she? You made it clear that this was nothing more than a business arrangement. You kept up your end of the bargain and so did she. Right?"

I nodded. Yeah, she'd only asked for a few charitable donations, one of which solely benefitted me. She'd been nothing but good and kind, sexy and sweet, and I fucked it up. All of it. "Why wouldn't she say anything?"

Dante shrugged. "Why would she? That's not what you want. Is it?"

Was it? "I want her." That was the only thing I knew. I

wanted Sasha and I would do whatever it took to make her mine. "I need to get out of here."

Dante, grumpy bastard that he was, flashed an uncharacteristic grin as he stood. "I'll make your excuses," he offered. "Don't fuck it up."

"Thanks man, your confidence in me is overwhelming. Seriously."

"It's just a bit of friendly advice. It's time to go big or get off the pot."

I frowned and a laugh escaped. "You might want to work on your pep talk, Dante."

"It wasn't a pep talk. It was a get off your ass and go get your woman talk. Go," he growled and shooed me towards the door.

I didn't need to be told twice. I loosened my bowtie and strolled towards the ballroom exit, ready to claim my bride. My woman.

For real, this time.

For keeps.

"Sasha!" The minute I stepped inside the penthouse my heart stopped. It was silent inside. Too silent for a woman who was always humming or talking to herself or listening to music. "Sasha?" I rushed down the hall towards her suite, frowning when I found it empty. Just to ease my mind, I opened the door to Dixie's room, which was of course empty since she was with Henrietta for the evening. "Sasha!"

I closed my eyes and listened to the sound of nothingness. Complete and total silence. My heart raced but I stepped back and went inside her suite, opening the closet and bathroom doors to check for myself that she hadn't completely abandoned me. Us. Her clothes still hung in the closet and lie folded in the drawers, her beauty and skincare items dotted her private bathroom.

She didn't leave me.

I rushed around the rest of the house, even to my office and the gym, place she never used even though I told her she was welcome to them. She wasn't in the kitchen either, which left one last place.

I took the stairs to the roof two at a time, going as fast as I could in my desperation to see her. "Sasha." There she was, still in that beautiful white wedding dress, sitting with her legs folded in front of her, a burgundy linen napkin tucked into the top as she ate a taco and washed it down with champagne. "You're still here."

She looked up at me with a blank expression on her face, the evidence of her tears were still present and I felt like an asshole. "Of course, I am. We're married. For the next two years anyway. What are you doing here?"

I shrugged, daring to move closer. "I live here."

"Right." She turned back to the taco, savoring the last two bites before she reached for the bottle of champagne and took several big gulps. Sasha unwrapped another taco and ate it slowly, sipping more champagne between bites.

She's here, I reminded myself. She didn't leave which was good. It was perfect, exactly what I wanted. Then why the fuck was I still so nervous? *Because she matters,* my brain answered the completely rhetorical question. "Sasha, I'm sorry."

She shook her head while she chewed. "Don't be." She shook her head again and swallowed. "The apartment is a good idea. As long as you're discreet then this won't have been for nothing." She didn't look at me but the thready nature of her voice told me she didn't mean what she was saying.

"Bullshit."

Her brows furrowed but still her blue gaze remained firmly fixed on the new taco in her hand. "Excuse me?"

"I said *bullshit.* You don't think the apartment is a good idea. In fact, I'd say you think it's a terrible idea."

Sasha shrugged. "Luckily for me, it doesn't matter what I think about it."

I dropped down on my haunches and plucked the taco and then the champagne from her hands, holding them in mine. "What if I wanted it to matter what you think?"

She sighed, trying to pull her hands free of mine but I held her tighter. "It doesn't. I heard everything and I apologize. I shouldn't have gotten upset. I had no right."

Dammit, I was losing her. "I wish you hadn't heard Jack saying all that shit," I told her, rubbing my thumbs against the soft flesh pulsing inside her wrist. "More than that, I wish I'd told Jack to shut the fuck up and for that Sasha, I'm sorrier than you know."

She tried to pull away again, growling low in her

throat when I refused to release her. "You are who are you, Alex. Your life is yours to live as you see fit but I think it'll be easier for both of us if we just keep things platonic when we're not in public."

"No, that's not what I want. Not at all. Will that be easier for you, because it sure as shit won't be easier for me."

This time she yanked her arms free with enough force she fell against the back of the sofa, before scrambling to her feet and putting some distance between us. "Yes Alex, it will be easier for me. This, what we're doing, it's madness. It's confusing and I'm the only one going to get hurt, so yes it will be easier."

I stood and removed the tuxedo jacket, flinging it absently on the chair behind me. "You're so sure you'll be the one hurt." Her words pierced my heart and I realized that I hadn't done a good job at all of telling or showing her how I felt about her.

"Yes. I am because it's already started and it's my own fault." She shook her head and turned away from me. "It's not your fault, Alex. It's mine. I'm not cut out for this, sleeping with you and living with you and then pretending we're in a relationship. I can't do it."

"Neither can I, Sasha."

She turned, a question in her glistening blue gaze that she quickly covered with a blank expression and a nod. "Good. Then we're in agreement."

"No, we're not." I closed the distance between us and

laid my hands on her shoulders, sliding them up her slender neck until my fingers were tangled in her curls. "I don't want to pretend, Sasha. Not anymore. Not with you."

She winced at my words and stepped back. "I understand," she said softly and looked away. "And Dixie? Will you still need me to be her nanny?"

My jaw clenched. "Are you listening to me at all?"

Her brows knitted in confusion but she said nothing.

"I'm standing here telling you that I don't want to keep pretending our relationship is real and you're worried about your job?" I shook my head. "This is un-fucking-believable, Sash. I'm trying to tell you how I feel about you, that I'm stupidly in love with you and you're talking about nanny shit." It was my turn to pace.

"You said you didn't want to pretend anymore, Alex. That sounds to me like you want to end the contract."

I stopped and turned to face her. Sasha was the picture of utter confusion. "You have no idea, do you?"

A tear slipped free and she folded her arms, notching her chin in the air defiantly. "I'll hold up my end of the bargain, Alex. I'll look after Dixie and pretend to be madly in love with you outside the penthouse, but I can't keep doing...the rest."

"Because you wouldn't have to pretend?" I took a step forward and her eyes widened.

"What?"

I advanced another step. "You can't keep sleeping with me because you feel something for me. Don't you?"

Arms folded, she glared at me as if she hated me. But she didn't deny it.

"Say it," I urged.

"No."

I took another step forward until just a foot separated us. "Say it, Sasha. Tell me that's the reason. Go on."

She pushed my chest, a move that sent her back a step. With a frustrated growl, she pushed me again, harder the second time around. "Fine, you want me to answer? Yes, okay! Yes, the reason I can't keep pretending is because I'm not pretending. I fell in love with you, which is the dumbest possible thing I could have done. I know who you are and what you want, most importantly what you don't want, but it happened anyway. So yes Alex, I'm in love with you and that's why we can't keep sleeping together. Or spending time together. Unless it's for your public image." Her chest heaved and just before she turned away from me, I spotted the telltale moisture in her eyes.

"Was that so hard?"

"Fuck you," she spat out in a soft, watery voice.

I laughed because my heart was full, because hearing that I wasn't alone in this made everything from this moment forward easier. "Sasha."

"Don't Alex. I don't want or need you to say anything. You asked a question and I gave you an answer. No further conversation is needed."

"Oh, but it is. You see, the reason I didn't shut Jack up when he was talking shit this morning before the wedding was because I couldn't." She moved to step away and I tugged her back to me. "His words shouldn't have pissed me off the way they did but the fact that they did made me come to an important realization. I'm in love with my wife."

"Alex," she pleaded and took a step back.

"Seriously. I should have been laughing along with Jack, smiling and planning for my secret life on the side. But his words brought me no pleasure. All I could think about was why would I want some puck bunny when my wife is so beautiful and sensual and lovely." I cupped her jaw and when she leaned into my touch, relief soared through me. "This is all new to me, being in love."

Her lips curved into a reluctant smile. "You've never been in love before?"

I shook my head. "Never. I mean not with anyone but myself." A bashful smile crossed myself. "No woman has been you, Sash. You're not impressed by my name or my money and you make me work for every smile, every laugh. I have to be me when I'm with you and, that's some heady shit. Being with a woman who just wants me? I didn't think such a woman existed. Until you."

"Alex," she whispered and held my face in her small hands. "I feel the same. Being with you makes me feel like I'm enough. I'm good enough and pretty enough, sexy enough."

"Enough?" I shook my head. "Oh no, sweetheart you are more than enough. In fact, I'm pretty sure that you deserve better than the likes of me, but I love you and I'll work every day to be worthy of the beautiful gift of your love."

"You already are, Alex. I promise." Her smile grew and she pushed up on her tiptoes, brushing a soft kiss across my lips. "Don't let anyone tell you aren't worthy. You're Alex Witter," she purred. "And you're mine."

I hooked an arm around her waist and pulled her body flush against mine. "Good because I love you, Sasha. So fucking much."

She smiled and her head fell back as laughter spilled from her luscious lips. "The feeling is completely mutual." And then because I could, because Sasha was mine, I lowered my head and captured her lips, kissing her slowly at first because I needed to take my time, to savor the taste of her combined with champagne and salsa.

She purred again and wrapped her arms around me, pulling me closer. Her tongue flicked inside my mouth and I deepened the kiss, devouring every dark corner of her warm mouth until her fingertips dug into my shoulders. The sound of the growl she emitted was so fucking hot, it was too much.

I pulled back with a smile. "Say it again."

"I love you Alex Witter."

Hearing those words from her lips made me feel full, like I had more love in my heart for her than I could contain. "I love you, Sasha Witter."

"So, we're doing this for real?"

I nodded. "Oh yeah babe, we are doing this. I'm gonna take you downstairs to our bedroom and fuck you until my name is the only word you remember. But first there's one wedding tradition you denied me by leaving early."

"Feeding each other cake?" She giggled.

"We can save that for tomorrow," I growled.

"Bouquet toss?"

"Fuck that, I'm sending it to Jack's office first thing in the morning."

That pulled another laugh from Sasha. "What, then?"

"Removing the garter." I wiggled my brows and guided her to the sofa. "Did I tell you how stunning you look in this dress?" It was big and puffy and white, showing off every inch of her delicious curves.

Sasha shook her head as my hands slid up her legs, under the skirts of her dress. "It's nice to hear," she whispered.

"I'll make sure to tell you how gorgeous I find you every day of our life together." I lifted the skirts and dove underneath, taking my time touching her silky smooth legs.

"Alex," she moaned when my knuckles brushed across her panties. "The garter is lower."

"Is it here," I asked and hooked her panties to the side, using my tongue to part her pussy lips.

"Oh," she moaned again. "Yes, Alex."

She was wet and delicious, tasting like salted caramel on my tongue as I lapped at her juices and sucked her clit. I wasn't sure I'd ever have her like this again but now, knowing she was mine completely? I took my time.

"Oh fuck, Alex, babe! Yes!" She jerked her hips and

when my tongue slipped inside her wetness, she pulsed around me and rolled her lips. "Alex, please."

I hooked one finger deep inside of her and curled my tongue around her clit. Seconds later a powerful orgasm shot out of her, making her legs quiver and shake as she rode out her orgasm.

With a satisfied smile, I fixed her panties and kissed my way down her legs, stopping only to tug down the garter belt. When I appeared with her belt in my mouth, the look of love she shot me stole my breath. "Who knew you were such a traditionalist?"

"Not me," I answered with a smile. "But there is one more to go."

Sasha frowned when I stood and offered her my hand. "The wedding night?"

"Fuck yeah," I growled. "But first I have to carry my bride across the threshold." She squealed and then laughed when I scooped her in my arms.

"Put me down, Alex! Your season starts soon."

"Hey," I frowned. "That's my sexy, curvy wife you're talking about."

Her expression softened. "Alex," she grinned and nipped my earlobe. "If you keep saying sweet things like that, I won't be responsible for what happens next." Her tongue traced the shell of my ear and my legs moved faster and faster, desperate to get her naked and beneath me.

"I love you more than I thought I would ever love another person," I told her honestly. "And it was our sweet Dixie who brought us together."

Her nostrils flared and heat flashed in her eyes, and the moment we were inside my bedroom, she stripped me down and dropped to her knees.

The sight of my wife taking me in her mouth while she wore her wedding dress? Forever burned into my mind.

And the perfect way to start forever together.

Chapter 32

Epilogue 1

The Honeymoon

Sasha

"You're seriously not going to tell me where we're going?" I looked around the empty private jet and smiled at my husband's attempt to surprise me. I glanced at the flight attendant. "Can *you* tell me?"

She shook her head. "I'm contractually obligated to secrecy. Can I get you a drink?"

My shoulders slumped dramatically but my heart raced with excitement and anticipation. "If I don't know where we're going how will I know what to order?"

Alex's lips curled into a knowing smile. "I know just the thing. Coconut pineapple margaritas. Keep'em coming, Luisa."

She nodded and disappeared behind a dark blue curtain.

I turned back to my husband and his heart-stopping smile. "So?"

"It's our honeymoon," he offered with a smile. "It's been too long but the season is over and-,"

"And you're now a Stanley Cup champ," I added, so damn proud of him.

His cheeks turned pink as they spread into a wide, proud smile. "A champ and a newly married man with the hottest wife on the planet." His brows wiggled and he leaned forward, pressing his lips to mine in a kiss that started soft and sweet enough, but like it always was between us, things quickly spiraled out of control. "How about I show you how hot you are?"

My lips curled into a grin as heat suffused through my body. My nipples tightened the way they always did when he hit me with that intense, dark expression so full of want and need. "Yeah, how are you going to do that?"

A voice cleared next to us and we pulled back, turning to the flight attendant. "Margaritas."

"Yes please. Thanks," I accepted the drink and turned back to Alex. "To being married to the best hockey player in the league, the best dad and the sexiest man in all of Texas."

His lips pulled into a pout. "Only in Texas?"

I giggled. "I haven't been *everywhere* yet." I screamed when he hooked an arm around my waist and pulled me onto his lap.

"Funny," he growled and nuzzled my neck and down

to my shoulder before he focused on the space between my breasts. "And sexy."

I tilted my head back to give him better access to my neck as a moan escaped. "Yeah, right there," I whispered.

He moved deeper between my breasts, his tongue left a trail of heat from the well between my breasts up to my throat and back to my lips. "You taste so good," he growled.

My body was on fire as he licked across my bottom lip and then the top. "Mmm, so fucking sweet."

I gasped and then shrieked when the cold liquid slid down my throat and chest. "Alex."

"I guess now you'll have to take off that shirt." He purred against my flesh as he swiped his tongue across the cold liquid, pulling a shiver from me. "Too bad."

"Whatever will I do?" I stood and handed him the margarita glass before I took off my shirt and dropped it on the floor. "Guess I'll have to find something else to wear." I turned and headed to the room with the bed, an extra sway in my hips.

"Or you don't have to put on anything at all, at least not for a good long while," he called behind me.

Laughter echoed behind me and in the next second his arms were around me and his lips were on my neck. "I guess that's an option too."

Alex spun me around, his gaze dark and hungry. "It's the only option. We have a few hours and I know exactly how I want to spend them. Inside my wife." He unfastened my bra and pushed me down on the bed, smiling at the way my boobs jiggled. "Beautiful."

"This bed is so firm and the bedding is so soft." I ran my palm over the soft cotton.

"Not now, Sasha."

I laughed and reached out, sliding my hand under his shirt. "This is soft and hard. I love it."

He shuddered under my touch. "Sasha, I'm trying to seduce you here babe."

I grinned. "Consider this part of my honeymoon gift. Come here, husband." I tugged his waistband until he was falling on top of me. "Yeah, that's much better."

His smile spread slowly. "So much better." His hips pushed forward and showed me just how hard he was for me. "So hot for me," he growled and then smashed his mouth against mine.

The kiss was the blue part of the flame, so hot that my skin was instantly slick and my heart banged against my chest. I was sure he heard it but the way he growled as he tore off the rest of my clothes, and the way his lips never left my skin was intoxicating. "Alex. More."

"I love it when you're greedy for me," he growled and kissed his way down my body before he settled between my thighs. "You're so hot. So wet. I can smell how much you want me."

My fingers tangled in his hair. "Good. Now you can taste it too."

He let out a low groan and swiped his tongue through my folds over and over, sending me higher and higher.

I writhed beneath him, every swipe of his tongue sent me into a tailspin of desire. It ripped through me with the force of a hurricane and I leaned into that sensation until it consumed me. "Alex, please. I need your cock."

He pulled back and smiled up at me. "I love it when that sweet mouth of yours gives such dirty commands." He kissed his way up my body until we were face to smiling face. "Again."

I wrapped my legs around his waist and rolled my hips. "Give. Me. Your. Cock. Now." His gaze was so dark, so sinfully delicious that I shivered. "Please."

"That's my girl, so polite." His jaw clenched as his cock head breached my opening, sliding deep and stretching me out spectacularly. "So fucking tight."

We moaned in simultaneous delight as he pressed deeper until he was fully seated. "Yes, Alex. Yes!"

He pounded deep. Slow and deep, a hypnotic rhythm that kept me perched on the edge of pleasure. His hips moved faster as his own pleasure increased and every stroke sent him deeper until he hit that perfect spot that made sparks shoot off behind my eyes. "You liked that."

I smiled. "You know what I like."

"I do," he grunted and did it again. And again.

"Yes, that. Just like that, Alex." My heels dug into his well-muscled ass as I bucked up, hungry and desperate for the orgasm that was just out of reach. "Please."

"I do love it when you beg." He pulled out—completely—and laughed when I whimpered in despair. Before I could tell him what I thought of his playful mood, he spun me around and lifted my ass high in the air. "So, so much," he moaned, punctuating the words with a smack to my ass. "I love it when you pulse around me like that. You're so fucking wet."

My body trembled from his dirty words and the way he touched me. "Alex." His fingers split around his cock and then down to my clit before I felt his thumb pushing against my back door. "Alex," I whispered.

"It'd be a shame to let all this moisture go to waste."

I laughed but it came out on a low moan as his cock and his thumb slid into me at the same time. The sensation was full to bursting but so pleasurable that I felt myself teetering on the edge of pleasure and pain. "Fuck, yes." I pushed back and took every last inch of his cock. "Yessss!"

He grunted and smacked my ass again with his free hand, still fucking both holes in a slow, drugging rhythm that pushed me closer and closer while never letting me fall. "I love it when your greedy pussy sucks me off."

"So. Dirty." Almost a year into our marriage and you'd think I would be used to his filthy mouth. I wasn't. And it never failed to get me even hotter.

"You like it," he accused and smacked me again. "I can feel how much you like it."

"Nope. I love it."

"I love you," he grunted, pounding deeper and harder, his hips moved faster as his cock expanded, telling me he was close too.

"I love you," I said back in a breathless voice. "Love

the way you love me. The way you make me feel. The way you fuck me too."

His hand on my hip tightened and he fucked me intensely, slamming into me in long, deep strokes that—finally—triggered my orgasm which was wild and explosive, a wildfire that threatened to destroy everything in its wake.

It consumed me completely. My hips moved on their own, still pushing back to take him as he pounded harder and deeper until his own orgasm roared out of him. I felt the heat of him as he filled me up and it served to prolong my own orgasm, or maybe it triggered another, I was so blissed out that I couldn't be sure. "Alex," I cried out as my legs quivered from exhaustion.

His hips slowed and his thumb continued to move, the sensation so wild and so pleasurable that my vision blurred. "That's right, baby, ride it out. I've got you."

The constant movement of his cock within me prolonged my pleasure until one last orgasm shot up my body and my thighs finally gave out. "Goodness, I think I'm dead. Am I dead?"

"I sure hope not," he whispered in my ear, slowly extricating himself from my body and falling to the side, pulling me with him. "Because we've got ten days in Jamaica to spend together. All alone."

I looked up, mussed hair interfering with my view of my husband's smiling face. "Jamaica? For real?"

He nodded. "You said you always wanted to go."

My heart slammed against my chest. "You remembered." Each day Alex showed me in another way just how good and sweet he was, how much I meant to him.

"Of course I did. And I even planned some things for us to do outside the bedroom."

My forehead fell against his chest. "SCUBA sex is still sex."

"I hadn't thought of that, but now I won't be able to think of anything but that until we do it."

Another laugh fell from my lips. "We'll see." I leaned forward and kissed him softly. "I love you, Alex Witter."

"I love you more, Sasha Witter. The day you showed up on my doorstep was the best day of my fucking life."

"How much longer until we land?" I was already on my knees and moving over his body.

"Couple hours, maybe. Why?"

"Because," I nipped his ear. "You've had a long season. Worked hard. Now it's time for me to be a good wife and take care of you."

That's exactly what I did for the rest of the flight.

After that flight, I knew I would never look at coconut pineapple margaritas the same ever again.

Chapter 33

Epilogue 2

Sasha ~ 2 years later

"Mommy!" Dixie rushed across the room with a wide smile on her face, her gait stilted but steady. She stopped in front of me and held out a cookie she'd pilfered from the table of goodies set up against one wall. "Cookie?"

I smiled and picked her up before taking a small bite with wide eyes. "Delicious."

"Good," she agreed and put her hand on my swollen belly. "Baby cookie?"

"The baby eats what I eat, remember?" I swear this little girl was going to be the reason I gained fifty pounds before her little brother arrived in our lives.

"Baby cookie," she said again and pressed the cookie to my lips.

The lights dimmed and the music began, a sign that

the game was about to start. "Ready to watch Daddy work?"

"Daddy?" Dixie had become the definition of a daddy's girl. She rushed to the door to greet Alex the minute he walked in, talked his ear off and became his favorite hockey buddy. "Daddy!" She pointed to the ice as players skated out, smiling and calling for him.

Alex had insisted on box seats now that I was pregnant, but I missed being in the stands with the fans, the roar of the crowd and the chill in the air.

"Daddy," she shouted when he stopped and waved to the box, his image displayed on the giant screen. Dixie waved furiously like she hadn't seen him just a few hours ago. "Go Daddy!"

The others in the box smiled at her exuberance before we settled in our seats to watch the game. The Highlanders dominated the last season, winning another Cup which made my husband's ego so big it needed its own seat at the table. This year they were favored to win again, but the season had only started a few months ago.

At intermission, the crowd thinned out and I stood to stretch my legs while the baby kicked like he was auditioning for the Olympic soccer team. "Settle down, you." I smiled at the energetic baby who never stopped moving but had made my first pregnancy enjoyable.

The door flung open and there he was, my husband. "Hey Sash." He flashed that boyish smile that never failed to get my heart slamming against my chest.

"Hey Witter. Looking good out there. Two goals in the first half, it's like you're trying to impress me."

He stalked to me, sweaty and still in most of his gear. "I know just how to impress you." He wiggled his eyebrows.

"As creative as you are, not even you can manage in all that." I motioned to all the gear that kept him safe on the ice.

Alex's eyes slammed shut and he turned his gaze to the man beside him holding a camera. A camera. "Don't curse," he said when I opened my mouth to do just that.

"What's all this?"

"This," he took my hands in his and kissed the center of each palm. "This is our anniversary. Two years," he said with so much meaning in his eyes that my heart slammed against my chest once again. "And I have an important question to ask you."

I frowned. Surely he didn't plan to reveal our agreement on national television. My smile smoothed into a smile at the reminder of our large audience. "You can ask me anything, babe."

"Excellent, because I'm asking for a do over." He held out his hand and the man behind him, his teammate Greg, dropped a velvet box in it. "I was too desperate to make you mine the first time around and I want to do it all over." He pulled the ring from the box and slipped it on my finger where the other ring already sat.

My eyes bugged out at the sight of the new ring. It was

stunning, a marquis cut diamond surrounded by amethyst and sapphire, birthstones for our two kids. "Alex," I whispered.

"Don't keep me in suspense, Sash, the whole country is watching."

"No pressure," I grumbled under my breath, which made the stadium beyond the window laugh in unison. "You want to get married again?"

He nodded. "I want to say our vows again. I want to see you walk towards me in another white dress. And this time, I want to spend a month in bed with you on our honeymoon."

I smiled and stepped in close, wrapping my arms around my sweaty husband. "You should've led with that hot stuff. Of course I'll marry you again. As many times as you want."

His mouth crashed down on mine and Alex kissed me with his whole body, his whole being, the same way he always did. He kissed me like it was the first time and when his hand settled on my belly where our son grew, one tear slipped free. "Love you, Sash."

"Love you too, Witter." He stepped back with a satisfied smile. "Now go bring mama another win." I winked and smacked his ass as he left the box, leaving the audience howling and laughing, having a great time as their favorite player put on one hell of a show.

* * *

THE END

Next is a preview of the next book in the series, **Curvy Nanny for the Nerd.** Enjoy!

Preview: Curvy Nanny for the Nerd

Brady Winsome is the genius behind some of the world's best video games, apps and other software. He's also notoriously private.

When a family tragedy brings his niece to his doorstep, Brady needs a nanny, one who's good with kids.

And secrets.

He thought he was getting a sweet nanny, one who wore cardigans and baked cookies.

Toni showed up with wild red hair, leather pants and a cherry red smile that woke up parts of Brady he thought were long dead.

And worse? She liked him. The real him. The geeky guy with the quirky sense of humor. She didn't care about his wealth or his status, just him.

It was amazing.
It was terrifying.

Chapter 1

Brady

Nothing is working the way I wanted it to, not today. Not yesterday. Not any damn day for the past year and some change. I can't concentrate. I can't focus, not for hours on end the way I'm used to working. It's why the first game in this series, *Shooter Alpha ONE*, was such a success and why the last three game series my company released over the past four years were equally successful.

My company, *Winsome, Lose Some*, has been my wife, my children, my whole entire life since I started at the ripe old age of twenty-three. I have lived and breathed this company from the very beginning, putting my heart and soul into every game, every app and every line on every fucking spreadsheet. But now? It's all gone to hell. I can't seem to string together enough time to make *Shooter Alpha TWO* even better than the first game, but I have to. I need to keep the momentum going because it's not enough to be among the top three gaming companies in the industry and it's not enough to be billionaire before thirty. I want to be *the* best.

I need to be the absolute best.

A loud shrieking noise sounded in the distance and I tried to ignore it and get back to the task at hand, tweaking the dialogue so it sounded more authentic. The research I'd done online and in person had given me everything I needed to improve it. Everything except time.

The damned noise grew louder and I pushed away from my desk, knowing that I wasn't going to be able to get anything done until I stopped that damn shrieking. I stood with a grunt and raked a hand through thick brown hair I hadn't done more than finger comb in too many days to count, steadying my nerves before I made my way out of my office in the back of the mansion and down a long hall that wound through the large living room and ended at the kitchen, where the noise was so loud I couldn't hear myself think. "What in the hell is that noise?"

Silver blue eyes that were identical to my own glared at me as if I was the cause of the offending sound. "It's the smoke detector," my niece Layla shouted at me. "I can't reach it. Obviously."

I ignored her rude tone and jumped on the counter to stop the smoke detector from making my eardrums bleed. "Better." I jumped down and stared at my niece through a plume of quickly fading dark smoke. "Now, what in the hell were you thinking?"

Layla folded her arms, flicking the blond hair she'd

inherited from her dad off her shoulders, and rolled her eyes with all the sass of a seven year old going on sixteen. "I was thinking that I'm hungry and since there are no responsible adults in this house, it was up to me to feed myself." She was being dramatic.

"You're being dramatic," I told her and glanced down at my watch to prove my point, but my eyes widened. "Four-thirty? It's four-thirty, why didn't you say anything?"

She shrugged but the look of disappointment in her eyes made me feel like I was failing at everything. "I assumed you forgot about me. Again."

My shoulders sank at her words, spoken so frankly and simply as if she just accepted it. "I'm sorry, Layla. I'm working really hard on this game and I lost track of time."

"Yeah, yeah," she said with a dismissive wave of her hand. "You're busy and important. I'm aware." She held up her hands. "I got it. You don't need to worry about me." Without another word she reached for the blackened grilled cheese and a butter knife, angrily scraping off the burnt layer.

I reached for the knife and she yanked it away, tossing it angrily into the sink and the sandwich in the trash. "Let me help."

"I'm fine," she yelled and stomped out of the room. She didn't run which somehow made it worse. Her controlled pace combined with her straight spine and squared shoulders was proof that I was failing more as a parent than as a game developer.

I felt helpless so I did what I always did, I went back to my office and buried myself in work. My sister was probably turning over in her grave at all the ways I was failing her little girl. Why in the hell did Marnie leave her kid with me, anyway? I was the awkward brother. The introvert who spent more time on his computer than with live human beings. Why had she, in her infinite wisdom, decided that I would be a good choice in the event of her untimely death?

Because it's been me and you since the beginning of time, she'd written in a note given to me by her and her husband's estate attorney, and she was right. Our parents died early and Marnie stepped up to get her awkward brother to college before she made her own dreams come true.

"Dammit!" Now I was distracted by thoughts of my sister and how she'd come through for me every single time I needed her. But this one thing she tasked me with—caring for Layla—I couldn't do it right to save my life.

I wasn't good with people, not even small people. Hell, I wasn't good with seven year olds when I was one and now? Everything I said was wrong.

Until now.

Layla was hungry and so was I, which meant this was the one thing in this moment I could do something to fix. I grabbed my phone and ordered food, enough for lunch and dinner for two hungry people, casting one last disappointed look at all the unfinished tasks on the list beside my keyboards. *Later. I'll get back to this later and I'll be* more productive on a full stomach and without guilt weighing me down.

"Layla," I called out from the other side of her bedroom door. The one thing I remembered about girls was that they liked their privacy and I respected that. "Hey Layla, can I come in?"

"Yeah, come in Uncle Brady." Even her tone sounded annoyed by me but I told myself it was what I deserved.

"Hey." I raised an awkward hand and smiled. "I'm sorry about lunch, honestly. I didn't forget about you so much as I often forget to eat but now that you're here I should do better. I *will* do better."

"Just buy some food I can make myself," she muttered under her breath.

"I did even better," I smiled proudly. "Lunch is here. And dinner. Sandwiches and fries, chips, salad and even a few slices of cake. Chocolate and lemon."

Her blue eyes perked up, reminding me so much of my sister my heart squeezed. "Chocolate and lemon are my favorite."

For the first time since I became her guardian, she looked like a happy little girl. "I know. Your mom's too. She would smash them together and eat them like that. It was disgusting."

Layla tossed her head back and laughed. "That's what my dad would say. Every single time."

"Care to join me for lunch?"

Disbelief shone in her eyes, but Layla nodded and followed me downstairs and into the kitchen. She piled two different types of sandwiches on top of a mountain of fries, grabbed a bag of freshly made potato chips and sat down. She ate without a word and that feeling of failure returned.

"Layla, I'm going to try to do better," I promised.

She sighed heavily as if the sound of my voice annoyed her. "It's fine, Uncle Brady. I know you didn't sign up for this but you're all I've got. I'll stay out of your way and you'll make sure there's food in the house I can eat. We'll be fine."

"Yeah," I agreed. "We will be. But to be honest, I expected to have my days free to work while you were at school."

She rolled her eyes. "I don't like bullies."

"No one does and I get that, which is why I need to do better. And I will."

She shook her head and sat back with a sigh that held the weight of the world in it, her eyes darting around the table. "I'll be just fine," she whispered, taking her cake and the rest of the food upstairs without a backwards glance.

"Damn!" I needed to figure something out. Sure, Layla was self-sufficient but she was also just seven years old and I'd left too much in her young hands since she moved in with me.

A babysitter. She needed a babysitter, someone who could watch over her while I finished *Alpha Shooter TWO*.

Now, can you order a babysitter online?

Chapter 2

Toni

"A refill, madam?" The Matre'd smiled at me as if he knew that the only way I would survive two hours of torture—also known as dinner with my parents—was with more wine.

"Absolutely. All the way to the top, Luc." I held out my red wine glass and nodded until I was satisfied that the glass was full enough. "Thank you very much." I raised the glass in his direction, smiled and took a big sip. "Delicious."

My mother was a stickler for decorum, as such she has never passed up an opportunity to let me know how much I disappoint her. "Was that truly necessary, Antonia?"

"Truly? Not at all. But he offered and I wanted more wine. What is the problem?" We'd barely sat down ten minutes ago and already she's found at least four things to criticize me about.

"You're looking good, sweetheart." My dad was the

nice one in the Stafford family. He always had a kind word for me and found happiness when his only child was happy.

"Thank you, Daddy. You look like you've been making time for tennis." His skin had a golden glow, his blond hair was sun bleached and he looked about ten pounds slimmer. Not bad for a guy in his fifties.

"Good, yes," my mother sniffed with disapproval. "But you've put on a few pounds, haven't you?"

Five things to criticize. "I am the same size I've always been," I told her as I rolled my eyes. I've always had a few too many curves for my mother's liking, and by a few too many I mean too many, period. She didn't appreciate my D-cups or my wide hips, even though they were separated by a small waist that gave me the perfect hourglass, if you're into that kind of thing.

"Yes well, you've always needed to lose a few pounds."

Six things. "I'm fine the way I am, thanks for your concern, Mother."

She gave me that heavy sigh, the one that reminded me I was a constant disappointment. "If you don't slim down you will never find a suitable husband, Antonia."

"It's Toni and I'm not looking for a husband, suitable or otherwise." She would never understand that while I was grateful for the life my folks provided for me, it wasn't a path I wanted to follow.

"A man wants a fit woman. Think of how much weight you'll put on after a few children."

I rolled my eyes. "Who says I want children?" I loved

kids, of course I did otherwise I wouldn't have become a nanny. But other people's kids were great because you got to leave them at the end of the day. Come home to more kids and nanny duty? No thanks. "And I am fit, Mother. I get plenty of exercise and if I a man doesn't like me the way I am, fuck him."

Dad grinned. "That's right, honey."

Mom gasped. "With that kind of language you won't have to worry about finding a suitable man."

"Good." I took a few more healthy sips in an effort to hold my tongue before I said something to my mom that I couldn't take back.

"Trevor Halsey is back in town after finishing law school. Suzanne said he's ready to find a wife."

"Good for him. I hope he finds what he's looking for." I didn't bother to remind her that I didn't know Trevor and had no interest in her friends' sons.

"Antonia, you cannot be a nanny forever. That's sad and worse, it's pathetic."

"It's an honest career, Mother."

"Yes, it is," she agreed with a glint in her eyes. "For women who have no choice, who don't have the options you do."

"I love my job and if you can't respect it, then I guess you don't respect me. Still." I stood just as our food arrived and finished off my wine. "It was so good to see you, Daddy. Mother," I growled and walked out of the fancy restaurant filled with Houston's elite with my head held high.

By the time I made it the few blocks to the parking garage because I refused to pay for valet, my mother had called at least a dozen times. I smiled to myself thinking how furious she probably was that I kept sending her to voicemail. I drove home, ignoring three more calls on the way, and parked my car before I made my way to my favorite watering hole just two blocks from my condo.

I called Lucy first because she was my closest friend. "Toni, I thought you were having dinner with your parents?"

"I was and now I'm not. You free for a drink or ten?"

As soon as she let out that sigh, I knew it was a no go. "Not tonight, Toni. Lena isn't feeling well and my boobs are sore. Sorry."

New motherhood was harder than it looked. "Don't be. Talk soon."

"Are you all right?"

No. "Absolutely. Go relax while you can. Later."

I stared at my contacts and knew I would get a similar answer from Sasha so I went with someone a bit younger. "Toni?"

I pasted on a smile and nodded even though the newest nanny on the Elite Nanny Service roster couldn't see me. "Hey Molly. Are you busy tonight?"

"Kind of," she hedged. "I lost my new placement because the mom said I was too tempting, so I'm trying to find a new wardrobe on a budget."

"Damn, I'm sorry Mols. Tonight I'm drinking but I'll be happy to help you tomorrow."

Preview: Curvy Nanny for the Nerd

"Really?" She gasped excitedly because I have the best fashion sense, period. "You sure?"

"Of course. As long as you realize nothing can cover up curves that spectacular." Molly needed to learn that her curves were not a statement on her sex life, despite what desperate housewives wanted her to believe. "But we'll tone it down as much as possible if that's what you want."

"It is."

"All right, see you tomorrow." I ended the call and stepped inside the dimly lit bar, finding an empty stool at the far end where I could be surrounded by people but also alone. "Double whiskey. Neat, please."

I needed to get a new placement. Soon. I didn't do well with a lot of free time, especially after another interaction with my mother. She poked and judged until I lost my shit, and I hated that she knew the exact combination to make me lose my shit.

My next gig would be better, I told myself. It had to be better than a negligent workaholic who kicked me to the curb for daring to request a day off after working twenty-one straight days. The guy was an asshole and if I never met another single parent like that again, it still wouldn't wipe the nasty taste he'd left in my mouth.

Or maybe what I needed was someone to leave a nasty taste in my mouth. I smiled to myself at the double entendre. Maybe I needed to get laid and that would take my mind off things, but looking around the bar all I saw were old timers who'd made drinking a profession, other sad bastards like me and the young but poor crowd in search of one night of fun. *No, thank you.*

Yeah, I needed a new placement and soon. Not because of the money, my trust fund made sure of that, but I needed to be busy. And if I didn't get one soon, maybe I would take off for a few months to a tropical island somewhere and work on my tan.

Oh yeah, that sounded perfect.

Chapter 3

Brady

"My philosophy is that kids are best when they are not seen. Or heard." Sarah, the latest interview to be Layla's nanny, not my next bedmate, purred the words through expertly lined lips and heavy lidded eyes. "Don't you agree, sir?"

My brows arched at the woman, grateful for my big oak desk as a barrier between us. "No, I don't agree at all. What are your qualifications?"

Sarah waved a dismissive hand in the air. "Oh, I have a kid of my own about the same age. I tell her to go to her room when mama needs some fun and she does. It works best for everyone."

Was this woman serious? "I'm in need of childcare and nothing else."

Her pink painted lips curled into what was supposed to be a sexy smile but it only served to piss me off. "It's my experience that sometimes men don't know what they need. Sometimes, they need a little push in the right direction."

"Wrong. Look Sarah, I'm only in need of someone to care for my niece and nothing else. Is that something you're interested in?"

She leaned back in her club chair, slowly crossing her legs to their best impact. "Yeah, sure."

That was not the answer I was looking for. "Layla, can you come in here for a second?" It went against my better judgment to bring Layla into this but I needed to give every candidate a proper chance. Right?

Layla walked in, her blond hair pulled into a bun on top of her head, dark jeans and t-shirt gave her a look of a child much older but to me, she looked just like my sister. "What's up, Uncle Brady?"

"This is Sarah. She's interviewing to be your new nanny."

The look Layla gave Sarah put a smile on face. "Is she qualified?"

"Of course I'm qualified, Lola. Why else would I be here?" Her smile barely reached her eyes and she arched her back to show off a mediocre boob job.

Layla glared hard at Sarah, arching a brow as she studied her. "My name isn't Lola," she snorted and glared at me. "No. Not her. Anyone but her," she shouted, arms folded as she exited my office.

I don't bother to try for a sympathetic smile. "This isn't going to be a good fit." The woman was more interested in my bed than my niece. I was sure she didn't know who I was but the house and the need for a nanny was a good indicator that I had money. "Thank you for your time."

Sarah stood, placing one knee on my desk and then the other, crawling across the large space until she was mere inches from my face. "It's probably for the best," she purred. "It's not good to mix business with pleasure."

My eyes bugged out of my head in disbelief. This was not real life. It couldn't be. I took a few steps back, shaking my head. "I'm afraid you don't understand."

"Oh, I understand all right. You're playing hard to get."

"No." Even if I was into playing games, which I wasn't, that wouldn't be one of them. "You need to leave."

She froze and then frowned. "You're serious?"

"I am." I quickly rounded the desk and headed for the front door, my strides long enough to put plenty of space between me and the ravenous babysitter. "Thank you for your time, Sarah."

"Your loss," she shot at me angrily, shrugging as she rushed out the front door.

At this rate I would never get this fucking game finished. I needed time, plenty of time. Hours of uninterrupted time to focus on all the fine details that would make my game stand out from all the other first person shooters on the market.

"It can't be this hard to find someone to watch my kid." I shook my head and went back to my office in search of a phone number I rarely used. A few years back when my company was just getting started, I did some freelance work for a big name gaming company and made friends with one of the players.

"Yo, Brady man, what's up? I thought you were dead." Alex Witter laughed happily, the only way he knew how to laugh.

"Why would I be dead?"

"Because I invited you to my wedding. To my kid's birthday party and even a coed baby shower, and you didn't even say fuck off, that's why."

I frowned. "There have been some, ah, developments in my life that have required certain adjustments, which is actually why I'm calling."

"I'm listening."

I gave him a quick rundown of my sister's death and the newest addition to my household. "I read about you falling in love with your nanny and I'm hoping you can recommend one for me?"

"To fall in love with?"

I rolled my eyes even though he couldn't see me. "Funny."

"Elite Nanny Service," he said and rattled off a number that I quickly jotted down. "She'll find you exactly what you need."

"Perfect. Thank you, Alex."

"Don't thank me. I'm planning an anniversary party for Sasha and I expect you to be there. I won't take no for an answer," he said before ending the call.

I stared at the phone until the screen faded to black. Alex

was a decent guy but he was far too gregarious and lively which is why we almost never hung out, but the number he'd give me was worth considering his invitation. Maybe.

"Elite Nanny Service, this is Serenity. How may I help you?"

"Oh, thank goodness. Ms. Woods, I was given your number by a friend, Alex Witter, and I am in desperate need of a nanny. As soon as you can send one over."

There was a long silence on the other end of the line before a well-spoken, sultry voice spoke. "That can be arranged," she said slowly.

"Oh, thank you! That's exactly what I needed to hear."

"But first I need you to come to my office for a proper interview."

My shoulders sank in disappointment. Of course this wasn't going to be easy. "You can't just send me a qualified nanny?"

"To a man I don't know and haven't vetted? Absolutely not." The woman sighed patiently. "It doesn't work that way, mister?"

"Fine, I'll be at your office within the hour. Is that soon enough?"

"Yes," she said with a smile in her voice. "That works perfectly for me. See you then, mister?"

"Brady," I growled. "Call me Brady."

"I'll be waiting," she replied and ended the call.

As if I didn't already have a shit ton of tasks on my

plate, I now needed to leave my house and worse, I had to interact with people.

At least one person.

As far as I was concerned, that was one person too many. "Layla, get dressed! We have to go out for a bit." Hopefully by the time we returned home there would be some plan for a nanny to start.

Soon.

Chapter 4

Toni

"Are you sure this is where I'm supposed to be, Serenity?" I sat in my car and stared up at the expansive brick mansion that was humongous but not ostentatious. Every detail I could see was functional and well-made, built for utility not for glamour. "This place could be a replica of my last placement." And that was the last thing I wanted to think about. Ever.

Serenity laughed, the sound husky yet feminine. "I'm sure. He's desperate and I think you are just what they need."

I rolled my eyes. "I'm not what anybody needs but I am damn good at my job."

"Be that as it may," she responded in that maternal voice that kept all the nannies in line, "Brady and his niece Layla could use someone with your particular skill set. And the address I gave you is accurate."

"Perfect. I'll let you know how it goes."

"I have no doubt this is the placement you've been searching for."

The smile in Serenity's voice put me on edge and I blew out a long breath. "anything else you can tell me? What he does for a living? What kind of hours should I expect?"

"Brady works at home so he will be there most days, but he'd rather keep the details under wraps."

I resisted the urge to roll my eyes once again. "As long as whatever he's into doesn't put me in any danger, it's fine with me."

"You'll be safe, Toni."

"All right, then. Wish me luck."

"Who needs luck when I have you?" Serenity ended the call and I blew out a long breath, staring at the oversized mansion until I gathered my thoughts enough to step out onto the long driveway and up to the imposing staircase.

It shouldn't be imposing, not when it's not as large as my own childhood home, but it felt like it was here for the sole purpose of intimidation. I didn't like it one damn bit, but I knew better the most how harmful it could be to judge a book by its cover. So I inhaled deeply, let it out slowly and rang the ornate brass doorbell. Twice.

Two minutes later the door opened and I really wished it hadn't. In fact, I wished I hadn't drank anything last night because now I wasn't sure if the person standing before me was the person interviewing me or a whiskey induced fever dream.

He was gorgeous. No, that was too tame a word for the sight of the man standing in front of me with thick chestnut brown hair and silver-blue eyes that were equal parts stormy and dreamy. He was tall, well over six feet, yet built. The corded forearms and strong hands said he was a man who take care of himself but the disheveled wavy hair and steel-cut jawline gave him a roguish quality that I found irresistible.

Staring at the beautiful man made me happy that I'd dressed to impress. My red leather jacket hugged my body perfectly, and the black t-shirt, blue jeans with the skinny red belt, gave me the confidence boost I needed to go up against another so-called master of the universe. I tapped my red knee boots impatiently and met his gaze head on. "Are you Brady?" *Please, dear god let this be a brother or cousin and not the man I'm supposed to be working for.*

"Excuse me?" His dark brows furrowed in confusion.

I sighed deeply. "Brady. Is that you?"

He blinked until his beautiful icy blue eyes focused on my face. "Who are you?"

"My name is Toni. Serenity sent me for a two o'clock interview." I could already tell this was a man who didn't bother with niceties or details. He worked hard and that was it. "Are you Brady with no last name?"

He nodded absently, looking over my shoulder. "The interview isn't until two."

"Yeah, I know. It's ten minutes until two."

Brady, or whoever he was, stared at me with knitted, dark brown brows. His pale gaze looked me up and down, assessing me carefully before his gaze landed on my face. "Okay."

"I'm here for the nanny position. Only the nanny position."

His lips twitched. "Come on in, Antonia."

"Toni," I corrected and stepped inside, ignoring the way his subtle, masculine scent worked its way into my nostrils before settling into my brain.

"Antonia is such a great name. Regal. Royal." He nodded for me to follow him and I did.

But I did not admire his long, lean runner's build. And I absolutely did not notice that his jeans fit as if he was sewn into them this morning. In fact, the moment we entered his office, I barely noticed him at all. The room was decorated in dark wood, black and brown leather with brass accents. It was a man's room, loaded up with books and computer equipment. "If you like the name, I'm happy to call you Antonia."

His lips curled into a grin. "Maybe the living room would be better," he said before turning and exiting his office, leading me back the way I came into the sparsely decorated living room. "So, Toni. Your qualifications are quite impressive."

Duh. "Thank you."

"How soon can you start?" His question was abrupt and coming from someone else, I might have felt suspicious, but I suspected he was just an abrupt kind of guy.

"Soon, but first we need to chat a bit more, don't you think?"

"Why? I need a nanny and you *are* a nanny."

I nodded slowly. "Parents who don't care about who takes care of their children, generally end up as problematic employers."

"Excuse me?"

I flashed a toothy grin, happy I'd gone for my bright red lipstick today. "What do you need from your nanny, Mr., ah Brady?"

He wanted to argue with me but thought better of it. "I need someone who knows children, someone who can work with a troubled little girl who is brilliant but struggling." He outlined her problems at school with a bully as well as her attitude towards her teachers. "She's a smartass but only because she's incredibly smart. She's tough and honestly far too mature for her years."

My smile softened. "She sounds incredible."

"She is, I think. But I'm not used to children and she needs help. I need a nanny who can help work on her social skills as well as her anger, but I also want to make sure she doesn't fall behind when she's allowed to start school again. It will require a one year commitment."

That was as close as a girl got to job security in this line of work. "Okay." Wow that was a lot of information in a short amount of time. "That's no problem. Anything else?"

"That about sums it up. Are you up for the challenge?"

"Sure. Can I meet her?"

He nodded, raking one hand through his thick, dark curls. "Layla."

A little blond girl appeared wearing black jeans, combat boots and a black and pink t-shirt that proclaimed her a clown wrangler. "You're the new nanny?"

I liked her right away. "Maybe. Depends on how we get along. You ever had a nanny before?"

"Nope. I went to school and hung out with my parents." She looked away at the mention of her parents and my heart ached for the little girl. Her gaze met mine again after a while. "I like your jacket."

"Thanks, I like your bracelets."

She smiled sweetly. "Can you cook?"

I shrugged. "Enough to get by. A big place like this doesn't have a cook?" It seemed odd but it wasn't my place to judge, at least not overtly.

Layla glared at her uncle in a look that clearly said, *"I told you so.* "I told Uncle Brady the same thing. He can afford it but he said no." Layla sighed like a long-suffering wallflower and I couldn't help but smile. "He won't be happy until I burn the place down."

Brady let out a strangled noise that was difficult to decipher.

I bit back a laugh. "I'm nobody's version of Iron Chef but I can teach you a few staples to avoid repeat visits from the fire department."

"Yeah?" Her silver-blue eyes shone with hope.

"Yeah, sure. It won't be fancy but it'll taste good and get the job done."

Layla studied me carefully, looking so much like her uncle minus the golden blond hair. "I like her," she declared and left the living room with a hint of a smile.

This was the strangest interview I'd ever been on and I'd had tons of them over the course of my life, but it seemed like it was done. Brady stared at me before he wiped his hands on his thighs and stepped back. "Can you start today? I'll double your rate for an entire shift if you say yes."

I resisted the urge—again—to roll my eyes at yet another rich dude who thought money was the only language they needed to know. "My normal rate will be just fine, Mr...Brady. But I will need to take a day off to pack up a few things sometime soon."

"Yeah, sure," he nodded but I could tell that his attention was already on whatever work he needed to do. "No problem." He stood, towering over me as he held out a hand to me.

I accepted the handshake but I wished I hadn't when the jolt of electricity flooded my veins. It was visceral, the connection that swirled between us, which was ridiculous since I didn't even know his last name. *It's just physical,* I told myself as I quickly shook his hand and yanked mine back, far out of his reach.

Far away from that uncomfortable feeling he evoked within me.

Far away from the urge to do something reckless. Something stupid.

Something dangerous.

Chapter 5

Brady

Progress. Nothing felt better than two full days of uninterrupted work, tweaking code and making adjustments to the story, updating easter eggs and offering better bonus gifts. Day and night for the past forty-eight hours, my ass has been in my comfortable, plush, ergonomic office chair staring at three monitors until my vision started to blur. I didn't sleep, didn't rest and I didn't eat a damn thing until I felt I made enough progress to reward myself with basic human needs.

The best part was that Toni of the full red lips and ever-present leather jacket, had everything well in hand with Layla. She was confident and competent, and there hadn't been one damn smoke alarm in two full days.

A yawn cracked my jaw and I knew it was time to venture outside my office and into the rest of the house. After a much needed stop in the bathroom, my stomach roared with the ferocity of a Grizzly Bear and I realized day three was halfway over and made my way to the kitchen. Before I even reached the edges of the space, feminine laughter rang out and the closer I got, the sound of music grew louder. It was a familiar song, one I'd heard hundreds, if not thousands of times during my youth.

"My mom loved this song." Layla. There was a smile in her face and when my gaze landed on her, the expression on her face matched. For the first time in months she seemed happy. Really and truly happy, as evidenced by the wide smile that split her face. "The Ramones just do it right, she always said."

Toni is still shaking her round ass to the sound as she whipped her hair around, a smile on her face. "Your mom was right, and she had excellent taste in music."

I held my breath and waited for Layla's smile to fall, for the tears to come but though her smile dimmed, it turned wistful. "She did. I miss her," she admitted quietly.

Toni stopped dancing as the music continued. "That's the part no one ever tells you, kiddo. The pain may lessen over time but you'll always miss her. This song will play and you'll think of her. You'll see a bouquet of her favorite flowers and you'll want to buy them for her."

Before Layla could ask another question, the loud buzz of the oven time interrupted whatever she'd been about to ask and offered the perfect distraction.

Both females squealed excitedly and bent over at the same time to peek inside the oven.

"Do you think it's ready?" Layla's question is equal parts hesitant and excited.

Toni turned to her and even from my spot at the edge of the kitchen, I could see her cheeks spread into a smile. "There's only one way to find out. Do we risk it or be responsible and give it another few minutes?"

"Risk it!" Layla jumped up and down, smiling when Toni did the same.

"Okay girlie, back it up so I can get this beast out of here."

My niece gasped when the dish came out of the oven, her eyes as wide as her smile. "It's so big, Toni! It worked. It actually worked."

"Of course it did," she answered with an easy smile that drew me in as much as Layla. "We make a great team." With the dish in her hands, she set it on the cooling brick and that's when Toni spotted me. "We made a veggie and nut meatloaf. Hungry?"

"Starved," I admitted with a frown. "Are you vegan or something?" Nothing on her resume said she was and I didn't care except Layla might not want to eat food without meat and dairy.

"No," she sighed as if she was disappointed in me. "But I do like vegetables and I think it's important to show the tiny humans just how great they can taste." Her gaze slid in Layla's direction as if to remind me of my charge.

"I love vegetables," Layla admitted. "Mom and Dad said that vegetables are better for the environment so we only ate meat a couple times a week." Her eyes landed on mine, the accusation heavy in them and I couldn't blame her.

She's been here long enough that I should know those details. "Of course. Your mom made us all eat vegetarian for six weeks when she was fifteen."

"Are you joining us for lunch?" Toni arched a brow when I shook my head.

"No, I should get back to work," I said just as another loud roar sounded deep in my belly.

Layla laughed first and then Toni joined in as she grabbed another plate and handed it to Layla. "Broccoli and sweet potatoes on the side," she said easily as if I hadn't just refused her offer. "Sit."

I frowned. "You're bossy."

"Goes with the job," she said, handing me a big bowl of sweet potatoes and nodding towards the small table in the middle of the room.

"This looks good. Thank you for letting me crash your meal."

Toni shrugged like it was no big deal and Layla rolled her eyes, just in case I was starting to think things had changed between us. "Your food and I'm pretty sure you haven't eaten in a few days. Have you?"

"Uncle Brady is too busy and important to eat," Layla offered in a snide tone.

"Oh yeah? How important?" She arched her brows and a playful smile formed on her lips as if she was teasing me.

"Not important," I rushed to answer before Layla told her who I was. "Just incredibly busy right now."

Something that looked a lot like disbelief flashed in her

bright green eyes and she turned her attention to her food. "Whatever you say."

"How long have you been a nanny," Layla asked, seemingly content to pretend I don't exist.

"Six years, maybe seven at this point?" Toni thought about each answer as Layla fired them at her before answering, which was a rare thing with most people and I couldn't keep my eyes off her.

The best part was that Layla's friendly interrogation gave me a chance to learn a lot about Toni without any effort. She obtained a master's degree in childhood development and early education in New York before she came to Texas for her first nanny gig. She's originally from the east coast and has a strained relationship with her parents. It wasn't much, but for some reason I was desperate to learn anything I could about her.

"What about you Layla, what do you do in your free time?"

She looked away, uneasy with the focus on her as she answered in a quiet voice. "I like to draw and I like to write stories."

"Like comic books or graphic novels?"

Layla's eyes went wide with excitement. "How did you know?"

"Writers who draw are a rare breed, my friend. I think it's incredibly cool and if you ever want to share, I'd love to hear what you're working on." She stabbed a spear of broccoli and shoved in her mouth, knowing that her easy acceptance of this hobby took the pressure off Layla.

She was, in a word, amazing. And more than that, her skills highlighted my own failures as I sat and listened, realizing that my niece was a complete stranger to me.

"Thanks," Layla muttered quietly and shoved a spoonful of potatoes in her mouth.

I ate a second helping of everything and when I was done, I sat back and patted my belly. "Thank you, ladies. I really needed that." Eating for me was mostly about giving me enough fuel to keep working but the meal was simple and delicious.

"No problem," Toni said and stood with a sigh.

My phone rang and I jumped to answer it, noticing the way Layla growled angrily at the interruption. "Hey Cal, what's up?" My creative director rarely called which meant something was wrong. I stood and left the kitchen, well aware that I was letting my niece down.

Again.

Or maybe still. At this point even I wasn't sure.

Chapter 6

Toni

"Where are we going?" Layla's question put a smile on my face because she was an incredibly curious child and the best part was she didn't have any hangups about asking questions. It was a good trait for a young to have, as long as you weren't the person tasked with answering them all. I didn't have all the answers, hell I probably didn't' have most of the answers but her curiosity made me want to find the answers.

"We're almost there," I answered her question without really answering it.

"Okay," she smiled. "Are we going somewhere indoors or outdoors?"

I shrugged. "Yes."

"Toni," she whined. "Will there be food?"

"They have food, yes." I smiled again at her grunted eyeroll.

"Are we going to watch something? To learn something?"

"Yes." I laughed at her impatient sigh. "We're almost there, little miss impatient."

"I don't really like surprises," she finally admitted. "The last time I was surprised, my mom and dad didn't come home."

"Shit," I blurted out. "Sorry. I mean *shoot*. That's totally my bad, Lay. This is a good surprise, I promise and I wanted it to be a surprise so if you don't like it when we get there we can do something else. No hard feelings. All right?" The little girl said nothing for a long time. "There's always more math problems to work out."

"Fine," she grumbled, a ghost of a smile appearing on her face.

When we arrived at the modern art museum, Layla was a little more cooperative. Her smile was hesitant but she couldn't contain her excitement as we went from one exhibit to the next. We went through paintings and sketches, watercolors and charcoal and oil paints, and through it all Layla was exuberant and excited, practically vibrating with it. "This is really cool, Toni."

I couldn't conceal my smile at her happiness. "I think so too," I offered. "I've been to museums all over the world with my parents and it was the best time I ever had with my folks." That was a sad indictment on my relationship with my parents, but it was the absolute truth. Dad didn't care as long as I was happy but Mom treated every excursion like a final exam that took some—but not all—of the fun from every visit.

"My favorite time spent with Mom and Dad was traveling with them for work. They made homes that were good for the Earth," she said proudly. "I always went with them but I was sick just before the last trip and they said I needed to stay home and get better." Layla looked away, her icy blue eyes filled with pain and regret. "I never got to see Norway," she replied with a choked smile.

My heart broke for this little girl but I was an expert. "What was your favorite place to visit with your parents?"

"Mexico," she smiled widely. "There was this little cabin they created that was completely sustainable. It was like living in a magic land and I wanted to stay there forever." The wistful smile on her face was contagious. I wrapped an arm around her as we walked from exhibit to exhibit, making sure she felt loved and protected.

"It sounds amazing and I'm totally jealous." Sure I've been all over the world at my parents' side but I never got to explore and enjoy the tourist spots unless they were on the schedule, which meant I got to see very little.

It took a few hours but eventually we absorbed every exhibit inside the museum before taking a break for food and water, and a bathroom. So far it was a good day, a great day even and I felt like I was making progress with Layla. Progress that would help her heal going forward.

"Do you have a boyfriend?" Layla's question yanked a laugh out of me over lunch because it was so unexpected.

Usually, in my experience, seven year olds weren't concerned with matters of love and romance.

I coughed to cover the laugh and shook my head. "No, I don't. Boy and men are trouble and I'm staying away from trouble for a little while." More like a good long while but Layla was too young to disillusion with the reality of the male species. She didn't' need to know about my most recent ex-boyfriend who sent me to a spa for my birthday, which upon first glance seemed like a thoughtful gift. Only when I arrived it was a weight loss spa, and instead of getting beauty treatments, he wanted me to fast and run and starve. I declined the diet portion of the weekend and overindulged in massages, masks and body wraps, taking full advantage of all the offers all weekend. When it was all over, I dumped him the minute I got back to town and I never looked back.

I shook off all thoughts of my past love life and smiled at Layla. "What about you, do *you* have a boyfriend?"

She let loose a giggle that was the sweetest sound I'd heard in a long time, shaking her head even as laughter spilled out of her. "I'm too young for a boyfriend."

"That's probably a good thing. Boys are trouble."

She giggled again. "Even Uncle Brady?"

Probably especially Uncle Brady with his nerdy good looks, premature curmudgeonly demeanor and sexy swagger. "Definitely, Uncle Brady too."

Layla laughed again, but soon enough her expression turned serious. "Do you think he likes having me here?"

Oh shit. "Your Uncle?"

She nodded.

"Yeah, I do. I mean it's an adjustment to get used to having a kid around, but I think he's learning."

She nodded, not quite believing me but desperately wanting to. "Okay."

I made a mental note to talk to Brady privately about making sure the little girl felt that she was wanted. I decided then and there that I would make sure Layla always felt wanted and loved, for as long as I was around. I leaned forward and flashed a smile. "Layla, I have a very important question to ask you."

Her brows furrowed and her expression turned serious. "What is it?"

"How do you feel about tacos?"

The question caught her off guard just as I knew it would and her little body shook with laughter for the next fifteen minutes.

Was there a better sound in this world than a kid's laugh?

In my experience, the answer was a resounding no.

* * *

Toni & Brady's story continues in Curvy Nanny for the Nerd.

Scan the QR code to read more!

Preview: Curvy Nanny for the Nerd

Also by Piper Sullivan

Nanny Series

Curvy Nanny for the Nerd
Curvy Fake Wife for the Player
Curvy Nanny for the Grumpy Single Dad

Small Town Lovers

Midlife Baby: Morgot & Grady
Midlife Fake Out: Bella & Derek
Midlife Love Affair: Lacy & Levi
Midlife Valentine: Valona & Trey
Midlife Do Over: Pippa & Ryan

Healing Love

Dueling Drs, Book 6: Zola & Drew
Rockstar Baby Daddy, Book 5: Susie & Gavin
Unfriending the Dr, Book 4: Persy & Ryan
Kissing the Dr, Book 3: Megan & Casey

Loving the Nurse, Book 2: Gus & Antonio

Falling for the Dr, Book 1: Teddy & Cal

Curvy Girl Dating Agency

Forever Curves, Book 8: Brenna & Grant

Small Town Curves, Book 7: Shannon & Miles

Curvy Valentine Match, Book 6: Mara & Xander

Misbehaving Curves, Book 5: Joss & Ben

Curves for the Single Dad, Book 4: Tara & Chris

His Curvy Best Friend, Book 3: Sophie & Stone

Curvy Girl's Secret, Book 2: Olive & Liam

His Curvy Enemy, Book 1: Eva & Oliver

Small Town Protectors (Tulip Series)

That Hot Night, Book 12: Janey & Rafe

To Catch A Player, Book 11: Reece & Jackson

Cold Hearted Love, Book 10: Ginger & Tyson

Hero Boss, Book 9: Stevie & Scott

Dr's Orders, Book 8: Maxine & Derek

Mastering Her Curves, Book 7: Mikki & Nate

Kissing My Best Friend, Book 6: Bo & Jase

Undesired, Book 5: Hope & Will

Wanting Ms Wrong, Book 4: Audrey & Walker

Loving My Enemy, Book 3: Elka & Antonio

Bad Boy Benefits, Book 2: Penny & Ry

Hero In My Bed, Book 1: Nina & Preston

Accidental Hookups

Accidentally Hitched, Book 1: Viviana & Nash

Accidentally Wed, Book 2: Maddie & Zeke

Accidentally Bound, Book 3: Trish & Mason

Accidentally Wifed, Book 4: Magenta & Davis

Boardroom Games

His Takeover: An Enemies to Lovers Romance (Boardroom Games Book 1)

Sinful Takeover: An Enemies to Lovers Romance (Boardroom Games Book 2)

Naughty Takeover: An Enemies to Lovers Romance (Boardroom Games 3)

Boxsets & Collections

Small Town Misters: A Small Town Protectors Boxset

Misters of Pleasure: A Small Town Protectors Boxset

Misters of Love: A Small Town Romance Boxset

Misters of Passion: A Small Town Romance Boxset

Kiss Me, Love Me: An Alpha Male Romance Boxset

Accidentally On Purpose: A Marriage Mistake Boxset

Daddies & Nannies: A Contemporary Romance Boxset

Cowboys & Bosses: A Contemporary Romance Boxset

About the Author

Piper Sullivan is an old school romantic who enjoys reading romantic stories as much as she enjoys writing them.

She spends her time day-dreaming of dashing heroes and the feisty women they love.

Visit Piper's website www.pipersullivan.com

Join Piper's Newsletter for quirky commentary, new romance releases, freebies and contests.

Check her out on BookBub

Stalk her on Facebook

Printed in Dunstable, United Kingdom

77997108R00173